Intro

I was thinking about what I could possibly write that would make you want to find out more about my life. I've pondered this question now for quite some time, mostly because why would anybody want to know anything that has ever happened to me? So, I'm just going to jump in. If you want to come along with me, then here we go.

Chapter 1

In the beginning was my first sentient moment. It was all about Bunny teaching me how to tie my shoe when I was three years old, and she was six or so. I can remember her teaching me to loop the laces, and then tie the knot. I can also remember her mother giving me peanut butter marshmallow chews, which were quite delightful. I would run over to Bunny's house, tie my shoes, and get a chew. The simple life of a child.

I was a happy child. I would love to perform in the Super-8 movies my dad was always taking. There is cinematic proof that I have always been a superstar. My dad said, "I never worried about Leslie. He was such a happy child."

I don't remember any of this, but there is proof of it on Super-8. I would run in a circle in front of the camera and laugh and dance to round out the performance. I think that there is also evidence of me doing this on Colonial Beach, where I got my first overexposure to the sun.

My next sentient moment was when I was four and a half years old. I was running around the neighborhood at my grandmother's house with a diaper on because I had blisters the size of golf balls all over my body. My parents in their infinite wisdom had decided to take my family to Colonial Beach, and left me under an umbrella, thinking there was no way that I could get burned. I don't remember being at the beach. I don't remember the burning, but I do remember running through the neighborhood in my diaper and being happy because my brothers were with me. We were laughing and having a good time, having fun, with blisters all over my body from the third-degree burn. It was a happy day because I was with my brothers, and we were having fun because I was running the streets in a diaper for all to see.

My parents didn't mean to let me fry on the beach on purpose. They were just having fun at the ocean, not realizing that I was suffering from the sunshine. They were thinking that because I was under the umbrella that everything was golden, and that there was no way that I could get a sunburn. The good thing about life is that I don't remember how horrific the burn was, or how much pain it caused me. Even now, I wouldn't realize how bad the burn was except for the fact that it was not the last time. Later when I was more self-aware, I do remember the extreme pain of sunburn. As a white boy, I would have to say that it is one of the worst things that could ever happen to you, because it just sneaks up on you. You don't think it's going to happen, but it does. The next thing you know, it's three weeks of pain, and there isn't anything you can do but wait to heal.

Chapter 2

My grandma was my guiding light, and in many ways the reason why I've never killed anybody on purpose. But back to my brothers. We were playing on the railroad track near Grandma's. My grandmother lived in Arlington, Virginia, which has one of the biggest train depots on the planet. She lived really close to an offshoot line that shot from her neighborhood clear over top of the whole Arlington train switching station. If you've ever seen the switching station, you would know that it was about a mile wide.

The danger at the railroad depot was the last thing on my mind. What was on my mind that day was following my two older brothers, Red and Francis, on the railroad track, running over to the big depot three blocks away. We continued to run on the track at the depot even though there was no escape, and we were 30 feet off the ground crossing over the depot. We were laughing and thinking everything was just so when we heard a train's horn blowing. We turned around to see the train heading right towards us, getting close to cutting us down like weeds. I could see the train speeding up as we were running towards it, and the engineer laughing sinisterly as if we were fair game to run over. "I'm so sorry to have killed them, but there was no way to stop the train. Didn't they read the no trespassing sign?" *Fair game*, he was probably saying to himself. *Open season on stupid white boys*.

We really all should have died that day. When we got home, Grandma asked, "What were you doing walking out on the railroad tracks that go over the entire Arlington train switching station?" (Oh my God, it's so big.) We were lucky to have survived. God must have been looking out for us that day, us three Dumas'. We made it that day.

It was that my grandma had taught us to believe in God. Each of us was praying to Jesus to get us off those tracks. It stands to reason that my grandmother, who loved God and knew God, was responsible for saving our lives that day. Thank God she was good because we should have been run over by a train.

"Well, how stupid could you be?" she asked. Apparently, we were that stupid. That day all of us knew there was no way off those tracks if a train was to come, and it came all right. I'm just saying that we all found God that day, not just me. My brothers and I, we found the Lord. He saved us, as we were screaming, running back to save our lives. That day could have been the end of the world for all three of us. Three kids knocked down by a moving train, severed into pieces right above Arlington station with their blood dripping down onto the tracks below. Deader than dead, all three. But as it turns out, we found God and jumped to safety as the train came roaring by.

Chapter 3

Well, I became a Southern Baptist, and if you don't know, that means that I get to go to heaven. Yeah, yeah, yeah, tell me everything you're thinking. We Southern Baptists have the only religion that matters. This is the single best thing that I got from my grandmother. I was baptized in the Holy Waters. I was dunked at 13. I don't know if I felt any revelation that day. I did have to hold my nose. Ricky Swartz said I was a pussy for doing it, but you know sometimes you just got to be who you are. I didn't want any water going up my nose, so I held my nose. They dunked me clear under my head and said some good words, and from then on, I've been living with God by my side.

We were so bored being at Grandma's for the whole weekend. I don't know what my parents were doing, but they were not paying any attention to us. That was for sure. They would leave us for weeks at a time. I don't know what deal Grandma had with them, but she was always looking after us. She didn't seem to mind, but we did have to go to church on Sunday. The only way you could get out of church was by being sick. Once we found that out, we were sick as often as we could imagine a way to be sick. If one of us was sick, another would have to stay home to care for the sick brother, because Grandma was not missing church.

My grandmother would have to believe that you were sick. Sometimes, she could figure out whether you were actually sick or not, and when you weren't, you would have to go to church anyway. "Get out of bed. We're going to church," she would yell at us. "Come on; you don't have a cold. You're just faking it. I can tell you're just faking it." You know, more often than not, she was right. You *really* had to be sick. You had to have a fever to stay out of church on Sunday.

As we got older, we figured out some ingenious ways to get out of church. Since you really had to be sick, Red and I talked Gene (my youngest brother) into screaming out the window the whole drive over to Grandma's house, just so we wouldn't have to go to church on Sunday. It worked. Gene must have been sick for two weeks after that one. Screaming all the way to Grandma's while Red was driving, hanging out the window howling like a dog. That's over an hour in the car. Red and I didn't know it was going to work, and Gene was going to get so sick, but, by God, he was sick. He got the two of us out of church that weekend. Gene got to stay at Grandma's house for another two weeks while he recovered from his illness. It was a bad one. I don't know how Red and I talked Gene into doing it, but we did.

"Oh," I said. "I better stay home and take care of Gene. Someone has to stay with him." I got to stay with

Gene. Red took the car back home. At sixteen he didn't have to stay at Grandma's.

Interlude

      I was just saying the other day that I surely do miss my brother. I lost Red to cancer eight years ago, and now at 63 I realize how lucky we were to survive our stupid days. I was watching Sam Elliott on TV just the other day, and he reminds me so much of my brother Red. If Red had only had as good a mustache, he would have been twice as famous. I am sure. He was the bee's knees, and all that too. Well anyway, it was fun to get over on Red because he was so damn smart. He was constantly figuring out ways to cross me, so I spent most of my time figuring out how to cross him back.

      I think I wasted my whole childhood trying to figure out how to be smarter than Red, but that just was not in the cards. He was the smart one. Then God, who I love, took him first. Maybe it doesn't pay to be smart. No one should be thinking all the time. Things just have a way of festering, the more you think about them. That just goes to show you that death is final. You cannot be relying on somebody else to do your thinking for you, because someday you're just going to have to rely on yourself. Nobody else should have to do your work for you, so get busy and do it. Quit being so lazy. "So, that's all I have to say about that," said Forrest Gump. I love Forrest. Forrest is my hero. "I didn't mean to start a fight at your Black Panther party," he says. I think I watched *Forrest Gump* over 50 times. I used that movie to inspire my students to write. I would give them a quote from the movie and make them write about it. Those essays were never boring.

Chapter 4

Of all the people I have loved in my life, I loved my grandmother the most. She taught me that life has its ups and downs. There are so many things that I remember, I will share some of those memories in hopes that you will love her too. Although she has been gone from my life for over 20 years, I remember her like I saw her just yesterday.

She always saw the good things that come from bad. Once when we were in her kitchen in Alexandria, I dropped a full gallon glass jug of milk on the linoleum floor. Instead of getting upset about it, she said, "Milk makes a good wax." She spread the milk out all over the floor and waxed her floor with it. She didn't complain nor hit me as my father would have done. She turned my dropping the milk into a good thing. It is this love that she showed me. Unconditional love. I have never forgotten.

Of course, my grandmother also took me to church on Sundays. I can't say that I ever liked it, but it did give me a background in Christianity that has stayed with me to this day. I was baptized as a Southern Baptist, mostly because of my grandmother's influence, because she was Southern Baptist. I took a dunking, and from that day forward I have been saved. I went to church with my parents, but it wasn't the same thing. I think it must have been the consistency with Grandma because we always went to the same church; no matter what, that was her church, Sunday after Sunday. She made a point of being there. My mother and father took me to church, too, but one week we were Presbyterian, next week we were Episcopalian, and the next week we were Lutheran. It wasn't until we went to a Baptist church that I finally felt at home. It seems like everything that my grandmother had instilled in me made me feel at home there, and I was once again feeling my Christianity. My parents continued to go with me to this church until we moved to Philly.

I am a good gardener because of my grandmother. I think that's one of the lessons in life that she taught me which I enjoy the most: how to care for and grow food. "If you don't get all of the roots, the weeds will come back," she told me. This lesson I have never forgotten. In all my gardening endeavors, weeding has become paramount. We had a garden beside her shed that was 20 by 20 feet, and we had to dig it up by hand. We grew all kinds of vegetables in there, even some pumpkins. Every October and November, we would take those pumpkins, stew them, mash them, and make pumpkin pie. I know how to make pumpkin pie because of my grandmother. She of course grew up in an era where you didn't have an icebox. Everything you did, you had to do that day, and eat it quickly, or it would spoil. She had a wealth of information to share with me, and I was a sponge, absorbing it all. I would do anything she asked me to do.

Chapter 5

My family moved from Permit Hills, Virginia to Kensington, Maryland when I was five. We were still in the DC metropolitan area because my dad worked at the Garfinkel department store as a display designer, but Gene was coming, and we needed a bigger house. My mom and dad were having trouble being a couple, so they had the great idea that having another baby would solve their problems. Has that ever worked?

The first thing I learned how to do in Kensington was cuss. I was cuss-free before, but I found out how convenient cuss words could be, and I was rattling them off like candy. "Hell" was one of my favorites. I'd be spouting Hell to everyone. My mom didn't care much for it. "Hell Mom, if my room is too messy, then get me my own room." I was blaming it on Gene. He was still in a crib, so it wasn't him making any of the mess.

That was the one time I got my mouth washed out with soap. I never cussed at my mom again. I was going to run away, but instead I hid in the bushes on the side of the house. It took my mom what felt like a couple of hours to find me, and she told me to come back inside. It was for my own good that she washed out my mouth. She had made some cookies and convinced me to come back inside and have some.

I didn't have to let her put the soap in my mouth. At five, I was already strong and could fight. I had two older brothers, and I was fighting with them every day, but I wasn't fighting my mom. That is one of the tender moments that I remember about my mom. Maybe it was the cookies. To this day I love cookies. Maybe it was the fact that she came looking for me. Maybe it was the fact that even though I didn't have to, I let her punish me. To this day I don't know why, but this is still a fond memory of my mom.

The first accident I can remember was when Gene was still a baby. All of us boys were out on a road trip in my dad's black '57 Chevy Nomad station wagon, one of the coolest cars ever built. I must have called shotgun because I was in the front seat beside my dad. Francis and Red were in the back seat with baby Gene. Gene was fussing up a storm and started crying, screaming, and kicking. My brothers couldn't calm him. This was way before car seats, so there was nothing restraining Gene from rolling onto the floor.

My dad took control and turned around while driving forward in traffic going through a construction site. On the left-hand side of the road there was a ten-foot ditch that was being excavated. Cars were going in each direction as we were moving on a two-lane highway. We were really blasting down the road, as my dad never went anywhere slow. He liked fast cars, and that Nomad was one of them.

When Dad turned around to help baby Gene, the car kept going forward. I wasn't watching the road. I was watching Dad care for Gene. The next thing I knew, we slammed into the ditch on the opposite side of the road. No one was hurt, but both side doors were pinned shut by the side walls of the ditch. Francis started screaming that the car was going to blow.

The Nomad had a rear window which rolled down. We all climbed safely out and onto the roof, and then jumped from the roof out of the ditch. The Nomad was totaled, but they really built cars well back then. The car didn't explode. It just went into the ditch. The smoke we saw must have been steam from the radiator. I don't remember how we made it back home. I don't remember if Gene stopped crying and fussing, but I do remember looking back at that car in the ditch and hoping it would explode like Francis said. You always want to believe in your big brother.

A few years later, Mom was pushing Gene on his tricycle. She had one foot on the rear runner. It was a large tricycle and built so that one person could cycle, and another could ride on the back. Up and down the street they would go. Gene cycling, and her pushing while riding on the back. They were having a grand old time. They looked so happy that I almost looked away, but I didn't. I saw my second accident.

For whatever reason, the front wheel of the tricycle just froze. It stopped completely like someone had put a stick into it. Now when the front wheel jams, all that momentum must go somewhere. I saw both of them fly off the tricycle and onto the sidewalk. My mom hit first. She landed on her face, and then Gene fell on top of her. Gene wasn't hurt, but my mom smashed her nose, and it was pouring blood. This was the first time I can remember seeing an adult crying. Mom got up holding her face and bleeding through her fingers. She ran into the house crying and screaming. Gene was laying in the grass beside the broken tricycle. Mom had put him into the grass before she ran into the house. He got up and we ran after her into the bathroom. Somehow one of our neighbors came running into the house too. I don't know how she knew, but Mrs. DeMarco helped fix up my mom.

Interlude

You learn a lot of stuff if you pay attention. You just have to be on the ball and listen to everything that is being said and watch everything that's being done. Then log it all, so you have it later when you need it. Then you can pull it back up and act like you know something. Life isn't that hard if you just listen, watch, and learn. Then do something, damn it.

It seems no matter what you do, you're still going to have prejudice. It's almost like human nature for us to hate somebody. We can't go through life without having some sort of racism, prejudice, or what I like to call a superiority complex. We are programmed to be divided. Humans have always been fighting each other throughout history.

I found out recently from an infomercial that I have an omnipotent superiority complex. That means I know everything there ever was to know, believing my thoughts are correct, making me smarter than others, and closer to god. Which I refuse to believe because I know I'm intuitive, but I have a lot to learn. I used to think Red knew everything, and I tried my best to learn exactly what he knew. That's why I am close to knowing everything, but you just can't fit everything into this little brain. I would like to think that I'm special, but as it turns out I know I'm just another run-of-the-mill human being with my own addictions, which I really am working on to this day. I am pleasantly surprised sometimes by my actions.

At this point in my life, my object was to learn everything Red knew because I truly still believe he was one of the smartest people on this planet. That became my first addiction, besides breathing, eating, and sleeping. I set out to learn everything I could from Red first, and my grandmother shortly thereafter. I learned to farm, take care of the land, to love God, and to love life from my grandma. From Red I learned everything else. I believe I lost my virginity in his presence.

My grandmother held Sunday school for all the children in her neighborhood. Her neighborhood became Black. My grandmother did not care. She had Sunday school on Saturday for those kids. She made sure that they learned the word of God. I'm not sure if she paid much attention to what happened to her kids after that, but she had cookies and milk for everyone every Saturday for 15 years, until she had to move. I have to say that I was always proud of her. Even though she has been my role model, my mama made sure that I grew up with racist White values and hated people of color.

My grandmother was kind of a saint. She made sure that people learned about God and didn't really care about the fact that all her Saturday school kids were Black. I always admired that. In my neighborhood, we were raised to dislike Blacks just because. I don't believe it had any justification. The truth is, Blacks and Whites are different. Now is that because we don't live with each other in the same neighborhoods, or is it because we're just different? My friend Fulton (my third Black friend) would say, "It's in your DNA. You can't help yourself. It's just the way you think about things."

Some people say they don't see color, but I pretty much see everything when I look at you. I can tell what part of the world your ancestry comes from. I can tell your nationality or see the mixture that makes you who you are. You can't really fool me. It's almost always the eyes, nose, and ultimately the chin that gives you away.

You can't hide from who you are. You might try, but that isn't going to happen. I can tell you who you are. I can still see what race combination you are. I can pretty much guess your race down to the quarter, and if you're four quarters, I usually get three of them right. I can't attribute this skill to my mama, but to living all over this country and paying attention to people's heritage. You see, I listen and learn.

You may think it is casual conversation when I ask you where your grandparents are from, but I am just wondering if I got your heritage correct in my mind. This world is so large that I'm thinking right now, Red didn't even know everything, even though I thought he did.

The two biggest influences in my life in making me who I am today were Red and Grandma. I'm so glad I had them both in my life.

Chapter 6

While we were living in Kensington, the highway department decided to connect Kensington with Wheaton, Maryland. We kids were incensed by this and tried to stop them from tearing down our woods. We took hammers, shovels, and pickaxes and dug what we thought would be tractor traps. We thought that we could get the bulldozers stuck, and they wouldn't be able to finish their highway, period. But guess what, a bulldozer can push down huge trees and easily fill in a 20-by-20-foot pit that we worked so hard digging. I don't think we slowed down the construction by even a day. But all of us neighborhood kids took weeks digging this trench with hearts full of defiance to stop the highway.

The highway was dug and poured out in concrete, and its four lanes separated my neighborhood from our elementary school. I wrote a poem as a fourth grader about how dangerous it was crossing the highway. They didn't put any lights up to control the traffic, and us kids had to cross Connecticut Avenue to get to school every morning. I wrote about how the cars didn't have to stop, were running us kids down, and killing all the kids. My teacher was so excited about this that she had my poem published in the local paper. The crime in all of this is that my brother Red and my mom really wrote the poem that I got credit for, but I took all the credit because it was only a good poem if a fourth grader had written it.

We talked all about how the cars would whizz by and run us kids down as we were walking to school. I don't think that ever happened, not one time, but I was always good at exaggerating. Even though the poem was not mine, apparently my mom and my brother were both good at exaggerating, too. In the end they put up a traffic light which allowed the kids to cross this huge four-lane highway safely. I think this wasn't supposed to be a devil-may-care intersection, and they would have put up lights at some point anyway. But even with crossing guards, it was truly unsafe to cross that highway before the traffic light.

In the summer between fourth and fifth grades, I learned how to play basketball. Tank and I would go to the elementary school and shoot hoops all day long. I got good, but I was under six feet tall. I didn't reach my final height of 6'4" until I was in my second year of high school. No matter how good at basketball I was, I was never good enough to make the team because I was so short. In seventh grade when I tried out for the basketball team, I was only 5'4". In eighth grade, when I tried out again, I was only 5'6". In ninth grade, when I tried out *again*, I was 5'8". It didn't matter that I could shoot 25 free throws in a row. What mattered to the coach was that kids were already six feet tall, and they could easily block my shots. It didn't matter that I had skills, and I could still make 50% of my shots. What mattered was that most of my shots were blocked.

I wish I had known then what I know now about basketball, because I would have leaned into my opponents and gotten more free throws. I was good at free throws. It wasn't until the summer between tenth and eleventh grades that I shot up to be 6'4". In one summer, it just happened.

Because I couldn't make the basketball team, I tried out for wrestling. In wrestling you don't have to be a big, tall guy. You just need to be able to pin people. I wasn't good at pinning people in the beginning, but I got better at the end. Ricky Swartz was my best rival. He was two weight classes above me all through junior high. We both got better and by the ninth grade were undefeated in our own weight classes. Both of us worked on being champions, and we rubbed off on each other. Ricky was my best friend next to Tank. I liked them both for different reasons.

In fifth grade I started playing tackle football without pads on Rock Creek's field. Us neighborhood kids in Kensington would play tackle football on the elementary school field. In fifth grade, we picked teams one at a time. Teams were generally equal. In sixth grade, someone decided to pick teams off the field and get uniforms and pads. People went with the team they thought would win. That year was a fiasco, as one team was vastly superior to the other. It wasn't even, and everyone good decided to play with the other team.

I joined the losing team, and I made everyone on the other team pay for their decision. We didn't win, but I trashed the other players. The other team got to the point where they wouldn't come anywhere near me. At 5'4" and 180 pounds, I could pound you when I tackled you. I can hear them crying to this day.

Interlude

I was talking to someone the other day, and I found out that life doesn't care about me and my opinions. Life has a way of moving forward regardless of our opinions. I got to tell you, though, that the older I get, the more opinionated I become. I have moved my hatred from people of color to a bigger topic: Muslims. My friends are telling me that Muslims are not all jihadists. I say, give them time, and they will take over our country and kick us out. Muslims are fighting an endless war that will continue until we all become Muslims. As a Southern Baptist, I just don't want to follow Mohamed. I'm for Jesus and loving my neighbor, unless you are Muslim. This is another way humans are being programed to be divided as I believe my religion is superior to others.

What is Heaven? How do we get there? Stephen Hawking didn't believe that God could coexist with the beginning of time, before the Big Bang. He said, "How could God exist in the nothingness right before the big bang?" I still believe. If God wasn't great, he would have a problem with nothing, but nothing was something to God. The good thing for Stephen is that a forgiving God may still let him into heaven. Stephen spent a lot of time in pain, yet he still was brilliant. I wonder if I could ever idolize Stephen as much as I do Red.

Chapter 7

I am an educated man. I have three master's degrees, and a bachelor's degree. My first master's I earned in the bathtub at 15, while playing with myself. Yes, this was the start of becoming a professional masturbator. All boys and most girls become masters of their own domain. It was after this first ejaculation that I started to become a man, with pubic hairs and all. I was a late bloomer, but as I became a man, I started to like girls.

My dad, mom, Gene, and I had moved to Philly as my dad got a job with Gimbel's department store. It was like my life was starting over. I went from 5'8" to 6'4" that summer. I wish I had known what masturbating would do. I would have done it sooner.

I became a ladies' man over the summer. I became a 6'4", sandy brown-haired, blue-eyed cutie. I still weighed 190 pounds, but they were stretched on a 6'4" frame. I was no longer roly-poly, but well-endowed. My frame was not the only thing that grew. I now had a bulge in my pants that all the girls were noticing. I had girls catcalling me to come over and talk to them. I really didn't know what to do with myself, or their attention.

I have always been shy, and I really don't start conversations, but I didn't have to.

First there was Julie Jacket. She was hanging around, and I liked kissing her. She had nice breasts, and she let me play with them. One day we were up in my bedroom on the third floor, and we ended up naked. The next thing you know, I was penetrating her. She squealed and said to stop. I was too big, and it was hurting her. Julie was my first. I came the moment I penetrated her, so stopping wasn't a problem. Julie must have told her friends what a monster I was packing, because one after another the neighborhood girls were lining up for my affections. I went from a closet masturbator to a ladies' man. I couldn't stop them from coming over. It was almost as though they were taking turns. Calling each other and lining up. I had almost every neighborhood girl that Julie talked to, but I wasn't satisfied. Even then I believed in monogamy. I wanted a girlfriend I could stay with.

Chapter 8

Bernie Bishop was my first Philly friend. His mother always thought that I was a bad influence on him, but it was really the other way around. The first time I smoked pot was with Bernie. After school we went to his house. He pretended that his house had an alarm when he opened the door. I told him, "Just because I'm a Southerner doesn't mean I am stupid. Just open the door."

We went into the basement and smoked pot. When his mother got home, he ratted me out and told his mom that I had brought the pot. Well, that was the beginning of her belief that I was teaching her son to be bad. I didn't even like pot the first time, but before long, we were smoking all the time.

About a week later, Bernie had a fight with his all-time best friend who lived up the street on Melrose Avenue. His family had a sports car and had parked it on the street with the top down. Bernie and I were going over to get even. Bernie had a crate of eggs. When we got to the car, he threw two of the eggs at the car. I didn't think that was anything, so I grabbed the crate from him and threw every single egg into the car. I don't know how they ever cleaned that car because eggs are impossible to clean. Bernie got his revenge, but when interrogated about the eggs, he said that I had thrown them. This might have been the beginning of my search for thrills by doing criminal acts.

Bernie and I would ride bikes and play king of the hill at the Grey Nuns' Academy, a Catholic school next to my house. Bernie was strong, but I was stronger. I was always king of the hill except for the times I let him win. I had to let him win sometimes, so he would keep playing the game. I would let him trip me up and push me down the hill every so often. One time Bernie was winning and climbing back up the hill faster than me, so I grabbed his pants and yanked him down. I tore his pants right off as he tumbled down the hill. I would do anything to win. He told his mom about that, and that added to my dark reputation.

One day while smoking hash on the Grey Nuns' football field, we were turned into the cops. The nuns must have seen us and called it in. We didn't get busted, but the cop took all the hash. He said that they had seen us lighting multiple matches, so the Nuns knew we weren't smoking cigarettes. The cop let us ride our bikes away. He didn't even ask us our names.

After I got my Chevy Nova at 17, Bernie got a Volkswagen Scirocco. His Scirocco had the loudest muffler that a car could have. It was only a 4 cylinder, but it would scream. My Nova had a 300 cc six-cylinder engine, but I maxed it out with a Holley carburetor and a racing cam. We would drive our cars on Curtis Drive, and he would catch up to me on every curve. His car was louder, but mine was faster. Bernie became a monster. He could pick up his Scirocco on the engine side while I changed the tires. It's good we stopped playing king of the hill just the year before because I'm not sure I could win anymore.

Chapter 9

On my first day of school at Cheltenham High, I had to ride the bus. I had always walked to school in Maryland. I sat with Bernie on the bus and figured out where my homeroom was and got my class schedule. Most people were being nice until I got to second period history class. I sat in front of this guy named Benny Gant and said hi to him before I sat down. The teacher took roll, and he heard my name and my southern accent when I responded. Before the teacher was done with the roll, he was chanting, "Less Lee, Less Lee" over and over. I don't know exactly what happened, but something in me just snapped. I got out of my chair and hit him in the face, then his back as he fell, and once again in the head, which knocked him out. I didn't give him any time to defend himself. I just went off.

I left the room and went down to the principal's office. I knew I was in trouble, so I decided to simply face it. The teacher called down to report the incident, and I was walking into the office as she was on the phone. It took almost a half hour before the other guy showed up. He had to go see the nurse first. It turns out that I had just knocked out the biggest bully in school. Seniors were afraid of him; he was so big. I got suspended for three days, on the first day of school, for fighting. Benny Gant got detention for teasing me.

When my suspension was up, I came back to school. I sat in front of Benny, and he still had a black eye. He didn't say anything to me in class. At lunch he and two other guys followed me into the bathroom. I was taking a piss when one of the guys pushed me into the urinal. I was caught off guard at first, but then I realized that the three of them were jumping me. I spun out of the urinal and side-kicked the guy who had just pushed me. He flew into the wall and grunted. I grabbed the next guy and slammed his head into the sink, knocking him out. Benny rushed me. I sidestepped and caught him with a right to the jaw. He went down hard. All three of them were on the floor. One was out cold. Benny and his friend were both moaning. No one else was in the bathroom, so I just walked out and on to the front lawn to let my pants dry in the sun. No one seemed to notice that my pants were wet, and they dried rather quickly.

I went about my day as if nothing had happened. Benny and his two friends ended up being suspended for fighting each other. They never told anyone that I was there, and they took the rap and a three-day suspension each. My seat was changed in history class, so I was nowhere near Benny. I never talked to him again. Strangely enough, no one else ever made fun of my name at school. Somehow, beating up the toughest guy at school was enough to fix that problem.

I had tried out for football that summer and had made the team, but when school started the principal told me that I was banned from extracurricular activities. I stopped going to practice, figuring I had lost that privilege. The coach stopped me in the hall one day and asked me, "Why did you quit the team?"

"I didn't quit. I was told I could no longer play by the principal."

"Well, we'll see about that." That afternoon I was back at practice and fully reinstated on the Panthers. I got to play tight end and earned my varsity letter. I guess when you beat the toughest guy at school, the coaches take an interest in you. I later lettered in baseball as a pitcher. The next year, I was too busy with work and making money to play either sport.

Chapter 10

I met Iggy Skinner at a pickup football game with Bernie at the Grey Nuns. Bernie introduced me to Iggy. He and Iggy had been friends since grade school. I found out later that Iggy was incredibly smart. I really got to know him in advanced calculus in high school a year later. I was in 12th grade, and he was in 11th. He used to piss me off because he could do all his homework on the bus ride to school. I was struggling to be smart, and Iggy hadn't seen a B in his whole life. Straight As, nothing but As.

At that game Iggy proved how tough he was. I have always liked tough smart people. All my friends have always been both. All my ladies have always been both. I have always been intrigued by people who can challenge my intellect and my strength; everyone but Debra. She was always very pretty, and she was my trophy wife. I was proud to be seen with her. She was a knockout, and strong, but not that smart. She was a kitten who turned into an angry leopard.

At the ball game at Grey Nuns, I had done something stupid. I had dropped a simple catch. I asked Iggy to kick me in the ass, and he did it. He kicked me hard. It hurt, but I asked him to do it, so I couldn't complain about it. He was the only one on that field that could tackle me alone. Normally it took three to five players to slow me down, as I was dragging them down the field. It was fun to feel unbreakable. It was good to be large and strong.

In advanced calculus, Iggy told me stories about growing up in Philly. I had already spent a year in Philly and was having trouble with a lot of the kids there because I still spoke with a southern accent. Some of the kids would make fun of my name, because it was considered a girl's name, but that didn't last very long. I've been fighting for my girl's name all my life while trying to prove that it is a masculine name. What a waste of time it was, because I ended up killing that bastard. He was such a fool and couldn't see the signs that his wife was cheating on him. I wanted so much to believe that she was loyal that I overlooked so much of what was happening. I killed Leslie after I discovered her infidelity and took the name Ed. I've gone on with the name Ed ever since.

Interlude

One of the things I learned in Philly was that there was no such thing as a fair fight. In Maryland you could cry uncle and the fight would stop. No one was trying to beat somebody to death in Maryland. We would even have school rumbles where people showed up with chains and knives, but no one ever got knifed or ever got chained. You would just fistfight. People did get hurt, but never killed at any of these rumbles.

In Philly, things were different. Philly fights were to the death, so I didn't want to get into a fight. The last thing I wanted to do was to kill somebody. The only fights I ever got into were when someone else forced me into it. I gave everyone a chance to get out of fighting. There was always a way out.

Because I was 6'4" and 200 pounds of solid muscle, a lot of my friends thought that I would fight for them. But if you started a fight, I would let you finish it. I would only stop the other guy from hurting you brutally if that was the outcome. My friends realized this and wouldn't push me into situations where I had to fight for them. It's a good thing, too, because I really do hate fighting, even though I'm good at it.

Chapter 11

Iggy and I became good friends. We were hanging out all the time smoking pot on the front lawn at Cheltenham High School. After Bernie introduced me to pot, I smoked all the time. At the time, Cheltenham had kind of an open campus, and whenever we could steal away and party all day at somebody's house, we would. If you came back for last period, you would get credit for being there all day. For some reason they didn't have an accounting system for all the middle-of-the-day classes. We figured out how to cut school, and we got good at it.

I was so good at cutting school that I often made-up excuses just to go somewhere. It didn't matter who was partying. If I found out about it, I was going, and of course, I took Iggy with me. He was a hell of a partier. The drugs never seemed to affect him, and he would still manage to get straight A's. I was struggling through school just hoping to finish, because I had spent all my time partying with Iggy and several of our other friends. I was jealous of how smart he was, but that didn't slow me down from wanting to party all the time. Once I found marijuana, there was no stopping me. If I could find some hash, baby, I was smoking it. I think that my whole senior year I smoked pretty much nothing but hash.

Iggy introduced me to his neighborhood friends. It was my second summer in Philly. Iggy talked us into hiking to Penny Pack Park. He got us walking down the railroad tracks to Penny Pack. He didn't tell us upfront it was a three-hour walk... one-way. "We will go camping. It will be great. We will have a big fire and have a good time," said Iggy.

It was a hot, muggy summer day, and we were hiking down the Elkins Park railroad tracks. We stopped at the Elkins Park Pharmacy and stole hot dogs and beans to cook later. When we got to the park, we were all tired of walking. Iggy of course was leading us because he was probably the only one of us that knew where we were going. I have never in my life been lost. I haven't known where I was sometimes, but I've always been able to find the correct direction to get back home.

Five of us made the hike. We all had camping gear, and we had food from the pharmacy. When there were four of us, we were traveling in force, but we had five, so we felt we were a force to be reckoned with. There were the two Toms, Robbie, Iggy, and me. We took over a section of the park, set up camp, and started a fire. After we set up camp and built a big fire, we started to cook the food we had stolen in a big pot. We had taken way more than any five people could have eaten at one time, but that didn't matter. We had a big old stew. We were getting high, and Iggy said to me, "You are the most wide-awake stoned person I have ever met in my life."

That has always been true. It doesn't matter how high I am, I notice everything. You can't get something past me, especially when I'm super-duper high. I could always tell when the cops were coming because I could feel them blocks away. I had an innate sense of when trouble was coming, so when all four of them decided to hump on the new guy, my Spidey sense was jumping. I didn't know these guys from Adam. I'd only known them for a couple of weeks. They were Iggy's friends at that point.

First Robbie, then Iggy, then the two Toms started humping me all over. My legs, my back, and my face were all being attacked. I'm thinking that I went into the woods with these guys, and I'm going to end up being a Philadelphia casualty. Another story of rape and murder. I went into protection mode, and mind you, at this point I was ready for action. I was pretty much a monster. I grabbed a huge stick and hit Robbie in the side of his rib cage, and then took that stick and rammed it into Tommy Singer and was just about to hit the other Tommy when they all screamed at me to stop. "We are just kidding around. It's just a joke."

I'd have to say that it was a good thing that I believed them in my half-stoned, crazed state of mind, because I was set to give them all a severe beating and leave them trashed in the woods. I didn't want to become a victim. Just like I thought they were going to do to me, I was going to do to them. All except for the rape part. I had no interest in guys. I've always liked women.

After that experience we all were the best of friends. You couldn't separate us. We became the Mud Sharks, and as a gang, we were formidable. We would leave our stencil everywhere that we went, so you would know that the Mud Sharks had been there. We started off as four and then became seven. I thought that we had become 27, but only seven of us got the tattoo. The others must have been wannabe Mud Sharks and not real Mud Sharks. They would hang out with us and party with us, but only the original seven were ever initiated, me, Robbie, Iggy, Rod, Jackson, and the two Toms. There were others around all the time, but only seven Mud Sharks.

We were ready to party all the time. Who wouldn't want to hang with us? One of us was always ready to get everyone who was hanging with us drunk and stoned.

Chapter 12

One night we took the party under the bridge, crossing the creek down by Iggy's house at the end of Coventry Avenue, right there in Melrose Park. We were getting loud that night, and there was one cop, Freddie, who just hated us. He wanted to catch us doing something illegal. Unbeknownst to me, Iggy, Robbie, and Tommy had been his nemesis, and for years he had wanted to catch them doing something criminal.

We were having a party in the tunnel under the road. There were four of us. It was summertime and hadn't rained very much, so the creek was clear, and the tunnel was dry. The neighbors must have complained about the noise. It was about 11 o'clock at night. Freddie came up, and I could feel him coming. I could hear what side of the tunnel he was climbing under the bridge, so we all ran out to the other side and dispersed. We ran in separate directions, and as far as I know, he didn't catch any of us.

It was just one example of him trying so hard to catch us doing something wrong that he couldn't wait for backup. If they had come in from both sides of the bridge, we would have been caught. It was his mission to catch us delinquents, and because I became a member of the gang, I too was someone he was trying to catch doing something wrong.

Chapter 13

The first Christmas we had together as Mud Sharks, I decided to buy everybody a fifth of Southern Comfort. Somebody else decided to buy some Boone's Farm, so everyone had their fifth of Southern Comfort and a bottle of Boone's Farm. We were partying in front of Iggy's house on the corner. Iggy had a cool house (well, his parents did). We could party there and watch the cars go by, but they were going by so fast that they would never be able to see what we were doing. We were smoking weed and drinking Southern Comfort and chasing it with Boone's Farm. We were all getting high, and that was when Robbie told us that he'd heard about a party. "We should go to this party."

We left Iggy's house and started walking. None of us was driving at that point. We were way past sober.

On the way to the party, four guys in a Mustang came driving up the road, spinning out everywhere, and not getting very far. It was just after Christmas, so there was a Christmas tree on the side of the road that someone had thrown out. Robbie picked up the Christmas tree and threw it at the back window of the Mustang. He hit the car — luckily, not with the trunk but with the branches, so he didn't really do any damage.

Four angry guys got out of the Mustang, and they were all bigger and older than us. They were ready to throw down over that tree hitting the back of their car. Well, it seemed kind of reasonable that they wanted to fight us, but at the same time quite silly. I guess because I was one of the largest, the driver of the Mustang came at me. Before he got within three feet of me, I kicked him in the chest as hard as I could and threw him into the air, knocking the wind out of him.

The other three instantly attacked my other friends. Each one of us was a pretty good scrapper, and I'd have to say that attacking us was a mistake. The driver got up after having the wind knocked out of him and ran as fast as he could back into the car. His other friends, who had been punched in the face, in the stomach, and kicked in the groin, decided that they would scurry back into the car too. Mind you it was wintertime, and the road was still icy. These guys weren't getting away very fast, so we ran along beside the car yelling obscenities at them and telling them to go home. We didn't know where they lived, but it didn't matter. We chased those boys off.

After that we came to the Melrose Country Club and decided that we could cut through the golf course to shave a mile off our trip. This golf course had a river running through it. It was a small creek, really. There was a sewage pipe over the creek and Robbie said to Tommy Spicer, "I'll bet you I can cross over this creek on this pipe."

Tommy replied, "Nah, you can't do it. You're a pussy. You can't do it."

Mind you there was a bridge in sight that we all were heading to, but Robbie was no pussy. He started crossing over on the pipe. This was wintertime in Philly, and there was a thin sheet of ice on the creek. Robbie fell off the pipe and into the creek. He got completely soaked. We were still several miles away from the party. We hiked double time the rest of the way.

By the time we got there, Robbie was freezing and shook like a leaf in the wind. He took off all his clothes, except his underwear. Somebody there at the house said Robbie could wear his long johns, so he took off the underwear and put on long johns. His clothes went in the dryer.

We all felt sorry for Robbie, so I told all the other guys that we should strip down to our long johns too. There were four of us at the party in our long johns to support Robbie who was running around in someone's long johns. Then other guys at the party started stripping down to their long johns. As though it was OK to copy us. Every boy at this party had stripped down to wearing only their long johns. Well, that made us Mud Sharks mad, and we started beating the hell out of anybody who was wearing long johns. Like only Mud Sharks were allowed to wear long johns. When you are a force, you can make the rules.

After we beat up one guy, the gal who was having the party asked us to leave. Luckily Robbie's clothes were dry by then. We walked home from the party kind of disappointed that we listened to her, but Robbie liked her, so we had to.

Interlude

It was during this time that I became a criminal. I learned how to deal marijuana and hashish by buying in bulk and selling to people. I think that the reason I never got caught dealing was that I was never greedy when I sold it. If I bought something for $6, I would sell it for $10. I never really made a lot of money, but people would buy from me, and then they would resell it, so I never had to have that many customers. I think this was what kept me from getting busted like my friend Rod. He would sell to anybody with cash. He didn't have to know you. He didn't care who he sold to as long as you gave him the money, and of course he sold to some undercover cop in Curtis Arboretum and got busted.

I never got busted. Buying in bulk just meant that I could get high for free. People could afford to buy from me and resell it and make a profit, so I was never really selling to strangers. I was always selling to people who were going to resell it to someone else. As it turns out, they were the ones that were taking the big risk. I never sold to someone I didn't know.

I had a guy I knew turn up with two people I had never seen before. They came to my house to buy some pot. I made the two people I did not know go back out to the car and wait for Gary to come back, so they would not see any of the transaction and only had hearsay. I was sure that Gary was trying to set me up. I always thought that he had been busted right before that and was trying to sell me out. Gary went to jail for three years, so I know he was up to betraying me to get a reduced sentence.

Chapter 14

My first vehicle was a Honda 350 motorcycle. One day after school, I was run into in the parking lot of Cheltenham High. I flew 30' from the impact, which was a good thing. I wasn't trapped under the car. My bike was. The impact crushed my tibia and landing on my head cracked my Bell Star helmet. I was laying on the ground knocked out for a while. When I came to, there were cops, an ambulance, a crowd of people, and Iggy.

I looked at Iggy and said, "Get rid of this." Somehow, I got away with passing him a tobacco pouch with four grams of hash and a pipe. Iggy took it and threw it far away. Even run over I knew I had to get rid of my stash before I was carted off in the ambulance. My broken leg healed quickly. The cast didn't even slow me down.

Just a bit later I was getting stopped by the cops every single day. I was certain that they knew I was up to no good, but they couldn't catch me doing anything wrong. I had bought a 1970 Chevy Nova after the motorcycle accident, and I took to bringing my Doberman, Cody, with me everywhere. She hated uniforms and would start barking up a storm at the cops as they approached the car. No cop wanted to search my car when Cody was in it. I was often signaled by the cops to move on as they approached because they did not want to face a vicious Doberman. Cody really wasn't that vicious, she just hated cops or anyone in uniform.

I had souped up the Nova. It had only a 300 cubic inch six-cylinder engine, which I tried to blow up all the time. I tried shaking it apart by red lining the RPMs. That car would scream, but no amount of RPMs would blow the engine. I ended up loving that car, and with Cody inside, I was fairly cop-free.

Rod and I had jacked a 327 out of a Chevelle that was left overnight in a bar's parking lot. We had stripped that car of everything, and I was trying to blow the six-cylinder so I could put that engine in it. I wanted to have a race car. After we took everything of value, we took the car back to the lot. Rod drove a tow truck, and we regularly stripped abandoned cars. The Chevelle's driver came back the next day to find his car had been stripped. That would teach him to drink too much.

Rod and I would do just about anything to make some money. After we would strip a car, we would sell the parts to repair shops for cash. We found dealing to be more lucrative and less work, so we spent a lot of time selling drugs.

Chapter 15

One time when I was hanging on the steps at the entrance to Asbury Park, I left my car unlocked with the windows slightly down while I walked to the 7/11. The steps were a hangout for me and many of my friends. Sometimes as many as 30 people would be hanging out there.

The police had been called because there were too many people at the steps, and that was one of the reasons why I had decided to go to the 7/11, which was just on the other side of Cheltenham Avenue in Philly. It had great ham hoagies, and I often went over there to eat.

Anyway, when I came back to my car, some cop had the door open and was rifling through my stuff. It made me mad that he thought he could go through an unattended car without a search warrant, period. His excuse was it was drizzling. "Who would leave their window open when it was raining?" he told his supervisor later. It wasn't raining when I left for the 7/11. That was just a flimsy excuse to be in my car.

I found out later that he was looking for pot, and that I, of course, was suspected of being a dealer. Even though I was quite careful, somehow I had gotten a reputation. At that time, I had long hair, and even though I considered myself to be a motorhead, I looked a lot like a hippie.

I've never been a hippie. I don't believe in free love, multiple partners, or someone else working to carry my load. I have always worked hard for everything that I've gotten in life. When I came up and saw this cop in my Nova, I got incensed. I yelled at the cop, "What are you doing in my car? Get out of my car!"

If you learn one lesson from this, remember don't you ever yell at a cop, unless you're Antifa. I saw that he had taken the oil rags that I used to clean my engine from under the seat. He had opened them to check them to see if anything was inside them. I was about ten feet away from my car, and he turned around, took out his billy club, and started punching me in the stomach with the butt end. He hit me about six times before I figured that was enough. I grabbed the club and took it away from him.

His partner, who I had just seen for the first time, was pointing his revolver at my head. He told me to drop the billy club. I looked at him, and I handed the club back to the cop who was beating me with it. He took the club and slammed me three more times with it. I was in fairly good shape at the time, and I was used to getting beaten by my dad. I also had survived a ton of fights with my older brothers, and neighborhood kids who called me a girl, so he did not even double me over

56

with his strikes. He didn't even knock the wind out of me. I grabbed the billy club again and the other cop put the gun right to my head. After they regained control, had me cuffed, and sitting on the curb behind my car, they realized that 30 people had witnessed the beating. I said, "You need to call your supervisor and get him down here. I am not just some common criminal that you can push around. I need to talk to your supervisor right now."

At that point the two cops were looking at me wondering what they should do. All 30 people on the steps that day had come down and witnessed the beating. It was a definite abuse of power, and both cops knew it. They called their supervisor to come down, and a full report of the incident was written out.

I tried to get the cop who was beating me fired, but all that happened was that he got suspended a week and six months of desk duty. I was happy with that. At least he would think twice before he started beating on someone else.

I didn't have any drugs or any paraphernalia. There was no reason to be treating a citizen with a driver's license and legal registration with the billy club.

He had no right to be in my car, and he knew it. I think that might have been what got him into more trouble than hitting me with a club.

He tried explaining why he was using the club. A 6'4" teenager was standing in front of him yelling at him. I imagine he was scared as I was yelling at him, and a crowd of teenagers were encircling him. He was close to 50 and not in great shape. As it turned out, I believe both of those cops learned a lesson that day. Some people don't feel pain. No matter how hard he hit me in my side, I didn't flinch. I bruised later, but I was a stone then.

That was the point in my life when I started distrusting cops. Until that time, every experience I had had with the police had been fairly good. In Philadelphia, when you get a reputation for doing something wrong, it's not just one cop who tries to catch you, the whole force starts watching you. It didn't take me long to figure that out. If I had been a slow study, I would be in jail to this day because there's no way that I was the upstanding citizen I was pretending to be.

Interlude

The sport I love best to this day is football. I'll spend all day Sunday watching professional football if I can. I hate it when anybody tries to pull me away from football. Although I have to say that lately, after football stars decided not to stand for the national anthem, I haven't watched any football. It wasn't until I found out that Russell Wilson of the Seahawks was helping children's hospitals that I decided that I could watch him play. At least he was someone who was putting out his own money. I feel like if you're making so much money playing a professional sport, and you don't help your community in some way, you are really cheating your community. When one professional athlete decided they had to protest the national anthem, I decided to protest watching football. It took almost a year before I went back, even though it's the sport that I like the best of all.

Chapter 16

We Mud Sharks played football every Sunday on Asbury Park field. We made it official by joining a sandlot league. This was when I began to believe that there were more than seven Mud Sharks. We had 20 people on our football team. We were good the second year when all of us became better at our positions. Jackson became a Mud Shark that year. He played defensive end. I played center and left linebacker. At Cheltenham I got to play tight end.

There were a lot of guys on the team bigger than me, so I didn't get stuck playing center at Cheltenham. I got in trouble for playing sandlot football on Sunday because sometimes I was so banged up that I couldn't move at practice on Monday. I ended up quitting the Panthers as I got my first job, and I hated being yelled at by the coach anyway.

Jackson was a good egg. He would get high and drink with us, but that first year I never witnessed him doing the crazy stuff. At a Lynyrd Skynyrd concert, Jackson was the top man on a three-man high where I was the bottom man, Iggy stood on my shoulders, and Jackson climbed over both of us and stood on Iggy's shoulders. I think Jackson had done some gymnastics because he wasn't afraid of heights. Rod and Robby started a fire with all the trash on the floor at the Spectrum, so we would have room for a three-man high.

The next year when I went to Lock Haven, Jackson wasn't such a saint. Iggy really started to have influence on him, and Jackson was snorting anything his friends came up with.

Chapter 17

Iggy Skinner was really the leader of the Mud Sharks. He wants everyone to believe that I was the leader because he would be in all kinds of trouble if anyone thought otherwise. But the truth was, if he thought about doing something, we would all follow him. One winter he decided to take us all spelunking. None of us had ever been before, but Iggy was sure that he'd read enough about it that he could do it. He got his father's station wagon (an old green Ford), and we drove all the way to the hills in Pennsylvania Dutch Country to go spelunking. Iggy, Robbie, Jackson, and I finally got inside the cave after we had passed through a very small tunnel. It was very claustrophobic. The tunnel led us to a main room, which was like a pool surrounded by land.

First, we got stoned and drank some Wild Turkey, and then we waded into the water to see who could hold their breath the longest. There was a light bouncing off the water and going back up and into a whole other space. It was an opening that was under the water that we just had to investigate. Iggy told me that when we were going from the first pool to the second room, I got stuck in the tunnel. I never got to see the second room and had to shimmy my way back out of the tunnel. I couldn't go forward. The others followed the light into another room. It was bigger, and the water was deeper and clear. They couldn't stand in the water, so they decided to go back to the room where I was.

We all got soaking wet. Not one of us took our clothes off before we got into the water. The room was warm, so we kept getting high and drank some more whiskey. It was getting late, and we decided to go back. The car was a mile away from the mouth of the caves. By the time we got back to the car, the water had started to freeze on our clothing and become very crispy. Our clothes were iced up, and it was getting dark. We piled into the station wagon and fired it up and began to peel our wet clothes off, running the motor in hopes that it would warm us up, but the moisture from all our clothing got the car to fog up and then completely ice over.

Now this was a Pennsylvania winter, the coldest time of the year. There was no way that we could see anything, but because we were all freezing, there was no way we were going to stop and wait for the car to heat up enough for us to get warm. Besides, the defroster wasn't working, so the windshield was never going to get clear. If we had been as clever as I thought we were, we would have put all our clothing into a shopping bag, so the moisture was contained. But no, we took off our clothes and were in our underwear riding in this car because we didn't have anything dry to put on. The heater was running full blast, but it was below freezing. We had wet the seats with our clothes, so the seats turned to ice. We had thrown our clothing into the back of the wagon, but it was frozen. Everything was frozen, including us. Even the car had been frozen all by itself in the Pennsylvania winter. Oh my God, anything you leave in the winter in Pennsylvania gets frozen. Even though it had a big engine, it didn't much matter. We couldn't get the car warm enough to get us to stop shivering.

Robbie was shaking so bad that he was having hyperthermic fits. That might be why I can't remember too much of it. (It was probably the mixture of hard liquor, pot, and the cold.) I had totally forgotten about this. My lifelong friends had to remind me that we nearly froze to death in the Pennsylvania Dutch Country. "Boy don't you know the Amish don't want you there?" said my inner voice.

We got to an intersection that led to the main highway, and all you could see through the main windshield was a little quarter moon (about 2 inches wide) looking out the driver's side. We couldn't see to the left or the right, so Iggy asked Robbie, who was sitting in the passenger seat, if the highway was clear. Well Robbie either said, "I don't know," or "No, I don't see anything." He really couldn't see anything either, so Iggy drove out onto the highway.

Kablam, we were hit and nearly tore the front end off the car. The radiator was steaming. The wheels on the front were askew going in both directions. We were hit at about 50 miles an hour, and we were at a dead stop in the middle of the road. Iggy, in his underwear, and the other driver exchanged information. Nobody in our car or the other car was hurt, so we drove on home from there. All of us still freezing in a car now that couldn't really roll straight. Jackson drove the 90 miles back to Philly in a broken car that should have really been towed and was all over the road. If we had we stopped the engine to wait on a tow, we surely would have frozen to death. Jackson drove because Iggy was out of character and could not bring himself to drive.

I didn't remember this event at all until Robbie told me why I hated spelunking. Robbie and I now both remember the windows fogging up bad. I don't remember the drugs or the drinking, but we didn't do anything sober. I do know that it's why I don't like to go spelunking, and I never did it again. Iggy always had us doing these off-the-wall, hilariously horrible, reprehensible, memorable things. My friends Iggy, Jackson, and Robbie had to remind me all about this trip. We again were knocking on death's door while having an adventure.

Interlude

I don't know if it's because I always had fast cars, or if I inspired my friends. I was the first driver in the whole neighborhood to have a fast car, so I don't know if they liked fast cars long before they ever met me, but all my friends had them eventually, too. Most of us had girlfriends. When you own a car, before you know it, everyone is bumming a ride. You get friends quick with hash, gas, or ass. Girls just like a man with a hot car. I've had many a father calling his daughter back into the house and off the hood or trunk of my car. "We were only kissing, Daddy," I'd hear my girl say on her way to getting dragged back into the house.

To still have a friend that you met when you were 15 is saying something. Iggy Skinner is that guy for me. I have other friends that came along with Iggy that I still keep in contact with: Robbie Harley, Rod Driver, and Jackson Walker. I have lost track of the two Toms. I became a man with these boys over and over. We did some crazy shit. I can't even remember a time when we weren't getting high and talking about what we were going do with our lives. When you have friends for 50 years, that in itself is an accomplishment. Through all our crazy adventures, we have all still managed to stay alive, unlike a lot of our other friends.

I have found out I truly adore women's derrieres. It has been so exciting now to be 64 years old and see girls exposing their whole derriere at the beach. It was worth driving all the way down to Florida from Washington after my divorce. I walk my dog on the beach and experience the delight of being 18 again. Although the only place there is anything happening is in my mind. There is little possibility that anything else could ever come out of my sightseeing adventures.

Chapter 18

Tulip Bishop was my first long-term girlfriend. Tulip was a gorgeous 5'8", blue-eyed blonde with a great derriere. I saw Tulip walking in the street one afternoon, and I found out who she was and found a way to make her notice me.

Tulip was new to the neighborhood. She, her mom, and her sister had moved into an apartment in Melrose Park near Iggy's house. She had already attracted the attention of two other boys. Somehow, I got her to notice me. I started picking her up from her Catholic school and taking her home. For six months I waited for her to turn 16, so we could legally be together in Pennsylvania. I was 19 when we first met and in college, so I had to wait for her birthday.

We were together for almost three years. I consider her my first wife even though we were never married and only lived together for a couple of days. We were both committed to each other, and she was a beautiful woman. I can still see her to this day as clear as yesterday. In my mind I can still smell her juices to this day. She was something. I should have never let her go, but I saw her bitchy side.

I was taking Tulip and her little sister to the store in the Nova. She let Sissy have all her anger. I don't remember what it was about, but I do remember that I never wanted that hatred pointed at me. I was beginning to have my doubts that the relationship was going to work out. I didn't know that fighting with a woman is part of a normal relationship. I was too young to know that you were never going to always get along. Normal couples can fight and still be happy. But who am I to give relationship advice?

I decided to break up with Tulip when my friend Debbie died from AIDS. She was Robbie's younger sister who I had admired from afar. I was spending time with Debbie's family rather than with Tulip because they were all hurting. When a teenager dies, it's hard to take. Tulip was fiercely jealous of the time I spent there and was hounding me to spend more time with her. I couldn't do both, so I quit Tulip.

I will say this though, Tulip is how I learned how to make love to a woman. She was the first woman that I had for long enough that I could experiment and grow my masculine member to entice her into letting me do things with it. It was a very exciting time in my life, no doubt.

Tulip later graced the pages of *Playboy* as one of 100 beauties of Philadelphia. They only got a side shot of her, so you only saw side-boob. She still was something with her long blonde hair running below her ass. I'm telling you, that girl was gorgeous.

I loved two women that made it to the magazines. My first love Constance was in *Penthouse*. I fell in love with her when I was five. I loved that girl for seven years. We both loved to French kiss and were kissing as often as we could. I have always been attracted to beautiful women. Some men will sleep with any girl who asks for attention. I have always been looking for the perfect woman.

That's another thing about me, I am a devoted man. I have only fallen in love with four women for any period of time. I seem to be able to fall in love at a moment's notice. I don't really need to know a woman very well fall in love with her. My lust is so strong, that I know I am compatible with this lady, and off we go into a carnival ride of sexual pleasures. At one point in my life, I hope that my brain realizes that love and lust are different words. But I must admit, when you're thinking with other parts of your body, it is hard to override lust and think about love. How is anyone able to respond correctly? I can't blame it on my manhood clouding my thinking, but I do.

Chapter 19

A little later in Iggy's driving career, we went into a Puerto Rican neighborhood in downtown Philly and bought him a yellow Galaxie 500 with a white convertible top, a beautiful car. The neighborhood wasn't all that safe, and when he got home to check through the car, he found a machete under the back seat. No telling how that got there.

We were testing this Galaxie out, just screaming down Highway 309, and racing anybody who would race us. That was one fast car. My dad had two Galaxie 500s, and they were built to scream. The first one got stolen. Damn, that was one fast car. I can't remember what they put in it. It might think it might have been a 460 with a 1200 Holley carburetor. Iggy's car would scream, so I think it was the same model with the 460.

Iggy and I were flying along late at night. Of course, we were doing our normal thing, getting high, and having fun racing cars. Somehow Iggy hit a curb, and we flew into the air and ended up in some bushes. We both looked at each other. Neither one of us was really badly hurt, so Iggy threw it into reverse and backed out of that guy's yard. All his bushes and wooden fence were dragged back into the street. We drove the rest of the way home leaving two big trenches behind where the car initially hit the ground and plowed into the bushes.

Chapter 20

Rod and I would go to the Spectrum every Friday they had a concert. We would both buy in bulk and sell to anyone with cash in the bathroom. I did this with Rod one whole summer. We would unload a pound every Friday night, an eighth at a time. It was easy until three Black guys were pushing Rod around in the bathroom. I was on the other end selling my wares and following Rod's lead. He yelled for me to come over.

We Mud Sharks had this special yell, that was to be used when we were in trouble. After the yell I came running. Between the two of us, we hurt those three guys fast and hard. Rod took the one nearest to him, and I ran at the other two, got them both by the head and drove them into the wall. They might be dead.

How could anyone want to get something for nothing? They learned a hard lesson that day. A free high is not worth missing the concert knocked out cold on the bathroom floor.

One time I was riding in a car with Rod just off Cheltenham Avenue by the 7/11. Rod, Robbie, some kid I can't remember, and I were all riding in Rod's Custom Demon. We were playing a game we all called, "scream chicken while you still can." It was a winter day, and there were patches of ice still on the roadways. No matter how hard the snowplows tried, there were still patches of ice left on the road. On that night we were all sufficiently high riding in Rod's 340 Demon, a monster car. The object of the game is simple. You drive the car and head it into a parked car, an oncoming car, a tree, a fire hydrant, a hedge, a fence, a bridge, or anything that was an immovable object on or near the road. Rod was good at this game because he had nerves of steel. We would all be screaming chicken as he was heading towards a parked car, and it looked like there was no way we were not hitting it. We were going 70 miles an hour and only 10 feet away, but somehow Rod would not hit the parked car.

Rod was winning the scream chicken game as everyone was screaming at the last one. It really looked like we were going to hit that parked car. We turned right down Godfrey heading downhill, and we were going towards another parked car at 70 miles an hour. We weren't going to scream this time, but dammit he got so close to that car that we all were screaming. Rod would laugh and then jolt the car back out to the middle of the street. That Demon responded instantaneously and got away. We were all swinging our arms and screaming like little girls. Screaming for our lives. We had made that dart back into the street, but there was still a patch of ice in the middle of the road. Rod wasn't able to recover and turn back safely down Godfrey; we were heading for a 300-year-old oak tree at 70. We plowed right into it. None of us had time to scream before that happened. The whole thing took about 2-3 milliseconds. Robbie was in the windshield-kissing position. Robbie always seemed to be in that position. He had kissed three windshields before this one and had the scars on his face to prove it.

Why Robbie wanted to ride shotgun is still a mystery to me. We didn't wear seat belts, so all of us became projectiles. I was in the back behind Robbie, and I swear I pushed him into the windshield. Then my head broke the window, hit the sidewall metal of the door, and bent it completely. The other kid broke his lip on the back of Rod's head and helped to push Rod into the steering wheel and then the windshield. All three of them were bleeding profusely. I didn't look like I had anything wrong with me, so the kid I didn't know said, "You need to get out of here. You're not hurt. There's no need for you to be here when the cops come."

We had alcohol and weed that we needed to get rid of, so I was happy to leave. Rod handed me a backpack which I later found had two pounds of marijuana inside. I lived on Warnock Street which was only about six blocks away. By the time I got there, I had a knot on the back of my head the size of a baseball. That was my second concussion.

I got away without incident, and without any police report. The Demon was totaled and had to be towed off the tree. It turns out the only damage to the tree was a 3' by 1' swath of bark from the trunk. Other than that, it hadn't moved an inch. Three hundred years was a long time for a tree, and it would have taken a much greater force to knock that baby down.

I saw all my friends two days later, and they were all still pretty banged up. I still had the knot on the back of my head. The night of the accident, I went home. I did the worst thing you could do when you have a brain injury, I fell asleep. I am lucky that I didn't go into a coma because I certainly had brain swelling. But I was young and stupid back in those days, and I was happy just to get out of there with no criminal record.

It was shortly after that fun extravaganza that I decided that I had to go away to college to get out of Philly. Iggy shortly went away to college in New York. Robbie soon went away to join the Marine Corps. Rod stayed in the area and ended up getting busted for selling drugs to somebody he didn't know. The Mud Sharks dissolved as its leaders had left Philly.

We stayed together for a couple of years playing Mud Shark football and going to hang out at each other's colleges. As it turns out, Robbie and I really got left out of everything. My college was too far away, and Robbie was in the Marine Corps and too far away. Jackson Walker had replaced us, and he, Iggy, Rod, and a couple other NY boys would hang out and party together at Iggy's college in New York. Everybody's life went on, but the Mud Sharks pretty much died out.

Interlude

I knew I had to get out of Philly before it killed me. I went away to college at Lock Haven where I enrolled as a computer programmer, but I couldn't catch on to FORTRAN, so I became a math major. This degree never really helped me except that it showed employers that I could finish something that I started, and I was good with math. I really wish that I had had somebody telling me that I was smart enough to be a doctor, lawyer, or even a college professor, but instead I looked for and found the quickest way to get out of school. Even though I started as a computer science major, I got out with a BA in math. My GPA was somewhere around 2.5. One semester I took 22 credits, just so I could get out of college that much faster. I felt like college was a fictitious world and had nothing to do with real life. As it turned out, that was true. My degree was nothing. The best that it did for me was a sales job, and a job managing a freight line. Not because my degree had anything to do with those trades, but because my degree showed my employer that I wasn't a quitter.

Chapter 21

College at Lock Haven was a great experience for me, but I continued to be a criminal. I would buy mass quantities of weed and resell it to my classmates. I got so bold at college that I started growing a plant on my windowsill. Thank God that plant ended up being male. The local police arrested me, took my plant, and displayed it in their office as an example of how good they were at stopping drug trafficking. Truth be known, that single plant was nothing compared to what I was really doing.

Those charges had to be dropped because of a technicality, anyway. The arresting officer didn't read me my Miranda rights, and I had to be released. I think that was the only way I avoided going to jail for that. That plant was just a symbol for me and everyone around me of what a delinquent I really was, living in what was known as "High Hall" among the dorms of Lock Haven. We High Hallers had a reputation to uphold, and I surpassed it.

The first thing I did at college was try out for the football team. I really liked tight end and left linebacker, but I ended up playing center. The coach was always riding me and calling me a hippie because my hair was long. He would also harass the three Black kids on the team. All of us were good team players, and we won our first game. But the coach decided that I had to cut my hair to stay on the team. I had cut my long hair before, when I was getting hassled by the cops, but somehow his demand seemed unreasonable.

The next practice I showed up with my hair stuffed into my helmet, so it looked like I had cut it. After we won the next game, I forgot and took my helmet off, and he saw my hair. He started yelling at me right in my face just like my dad would do. That was the last time I played for him. Two of the Black players quit that week too. After I left, most of his anger landed on them. The team never won another game after that. Good football players went to Penn State and somehow knew to avoid that redneck coach.

I next went to wrestling intramurals and did so well that I had to face our state champion. He beat me, but it was really on a technicality. It wasn't because he outwrestled me. He put me into a figure four leg lockout which was what I called it when your opponent puts his butthole right over your face. He hadn't washed in at least two days, and it stank like hell. I did the only thing a street fighter could do. I bit him, and I bit him hard. He jumped off me, and I got control of him and was leaning towards pinning him. He kept screaming and screaming, "He bit me. He bit me. He bit me."

I said, "I didn't bite you." But as it turns out, I broke the skin, and there was an indentation from my teeth on his leg. Needless to say, I was banned from wrestling in college after that. I don't think that his move ought to be legal because he purposefully didn't bathe for several days before he put his butthole over my face. He was asking for somebody to bite him.

That was his signature move, I found out later. He was very successful with it. It was one of the reasons he was a state champion. I really think it was because he smelled like shit, and he put his asshole over everybody's face and killed them. They couldn't breathe. That was how he won wrestling matches.

I continued to deal pot at college. I've always liked the idea of other people paying for my high. The worst thing that I did in school was that I got a hold of some synthetic THC. Because of my belief in selling things cheaply to people, a lot of people I sold this to ended up dead, near dead, going crazy, and losing their minds. This drug was serious.

The synthetic THC was really a truth serum that the government had developed to use when interrogating prisoners. A friend of mine sold it to me dirt cheap, just trying to get rid of it. The story goes that it was stolen from the Feds. I had so much of it that I was selling grams of it for about 20 bucks. Because it was so cheap, people wouldn't respect the drug. I told everyone I sold it to that you only need a pinch to get high, but people would do the whole gram. Some of those people had cardiac arrest, bouts of mental illness, or just overdosed. I had my whole drug network helping me to sell this drug. Iggy told me that he was selling it in New York for 150 a gram. I always felt bad about so many people getting hurt by this drug, but I warned everybody. It was a nasty drug.

I carry the scars of selling that drug on my face. Even though I was practically giving this THC away, one kid still tried to steal it from me. I decided to fight him because I thought I was a badass. I'm not afraid of a knife. Early in my studies of Taekwondo, I learned how to take care of a man with a weapon. He still managed to cut me. That pretty much started a gang war as my people went to war with his side, and even more people died over this drug. As it turns out, greed is a terrible thing. Even though I was practically giving that shit away, people still tried to get it for free. The boy who knifed me ended up dead. A neighborhood gang heard about it and couldn't allow him to live. A couple of his lieutenants had to go too, but that's only because they were supporting him. If they had let him go, I'm sure they'd still be alive to talk about it.

Interlude

The one thing I learned from my criminal experience is that every dollar that I made illegally was taken away from me. God wouldn't let me keep a penny of it. I got into accidents and wrecked my Nova three or four times and the Road Runner twice. I had the money to put them back together, but then I would wreck them again. It wasn't that I was a bad driver so much as it was God punishing me for making money by dealing. I bought the Blue Mule, a tractor, with Rod's and my drug money. Bernie Bishop talked me into it, and we became professional drivers with the Blue Mule. I blew up the engine in Texas when I missed a shift and over revved the engine. God really turned me around and taught me a valuable lesson. After He took the truck, I was never a criminal again. I learned my lesson without having to go to jail. (Thank-you God.)

I've always known that God loves me. He proved it when I was a child running over the railroad tracks at the Alexandria Train Depot with my brothers. He has proved it a lot of other times too when I could have been dead, but I lived. He's given me little voices that resound in my head, and those voices have saved me. They have prevented me from running right into deer on the highway in front of me. When the guy tried to knife me in the neck, His voice told me to bend backward to keep the knife from cutting my throat. These voices told me not to worry about my wallet when I had lost it because it was going to be returned to me. It is my belief in God that has helped me through so many hard times.

Chapter 22

One time while at college in 1976, I thought I loved this girl. But she would not love me back, and it made my heart hurt so bad. I took my Nova on a mountainous road that follows Lock Haven River. I was driving way too fast on an icy road in the wintertime. I thought I loved her so much that I was going to drive off that roadway. I was going almost 80, and I thought I would just fly into the ravine, 500 feet below into the Lock Haven River. After about 10 minutes of driving super-fast and risking my life on the icy road, I thought better of killing myself. I started slowing the car down to about 60. I saw a turnout on the side where I could turn the car around and head back into town and safety. Guess what, that whole turn off was just one big ice pit. There was no traction anywhere, and I was still doing 60, expecting to be able to slow down enough to turn around and go back. Somehow, I skidded to a stop. I didn't hit the guardrail and fly through like I had envisioned in my mind. I was saved that day. This wasn't the first time that my life had been saved for me when I was doing something stupid, and it wouldn't be the last.

The moral to this story is, "Don't tempt the gods." I know I said God loves me, but I had started saying that I was going to kill myself. I was going to be a dead soul, and all those gods (fallen angels) were waiting for me to crossover to the other side. They were furious with me when they didn't get a chance to take me. When I had changed my mind and decided that I was going to live, they wanted my soul. I will say that my God saved me that day and allowed me to continue with my life by stopping the Nova. I was destined for some great things to come later in life. My God saved me from the clutches of the other gods and stopped my car.

Interlude

I have three life lessons that we all could live by, and I think there are as important as the 10 commandments. My three life-expanding lessons:
#1 Don't tempt the gods.
#2 Avoid pain.
#3 Seek happiness.

I have found that these lessons are good for everyone I love to live by. I was not the only crazy one in my group. Iggy still to this day likes to challenge his life. He's always been into rock climbing, and of course since Iggy is brilliant, he has always been very good at it too. But being very good at it has caused him to tackle some 5.11 at the Gunks, the Colorado Rockies, and anywhere he could go where they exist. A 5.11 is a hard climb where you must go upside down and hold all your weight with one hand or one hold while you're climbing vertically, horizontally, and then vertically again. It's almost like jumping off a ledge and catching another ledge 10 feet away, like Rambo or Jackie Chan.

Jackie Chan does all his own stunts. He doesn't believe in stand-ins. He forgot to abide by my lessons. One day the gods almost took him when he slipped during an impossible stunt. My favorite action hero may ultimately die doing one of his own stunts. Anyway, Iggy is still an amazing climber, and I went with him quite a few times, as did many of my other friends. He was the only one that I would trust to go climbing with. I have never climbed with anyone else. I trusted him implicitly.

He always had to go first, so I could watch and see where the handholds were, and it wouldn't be as much work for me. Frankly, holding onto the side of a mountainous wall is extremely scary to me, and I never would have done it without Iggy. I wrote my life lessons for Iggy. He is always risking his life. He almost died on a rock face in Boulder when the cliff chopped out a piece of his hamstring as he was falling, and he nearly bled to death. God loves
Iggy too.

Chapter 23

My second love was Marjorie Tyler. Marjorie and I were like peas and carrots (just like Forrest Gump and Jenny). From the moment I declared my love for her, we were inseparable. She started living with me in my Fern Rock one-bedroom apartment. It had a garage for the Road Runner, my new monster. I got the bottom two floors of a three-story row house. I would park the Nova in the driveway, and only bring the Road Runner out on Saturday nights after I tuned it by ear for racing.

We were like two cats in heat. I don't think there was a time when we weren't doing it in some part of the apartment. I even converted a storage room into another bedroom because we would be a floor away from our neighbors. They were also abnormal sex fiends. It was cooler in the summer and warmer in the winter.

My first step into independence was with Marjorie. My dad told me to get out of his house for taking a shower with her, so I found an apartment, and three days later I was out of his house and living with Marjorie. Francis told my dad that he had kicked me out because he was so jealous of Marjorie's titties, and that is why Dad told me to get out. Marjorie was a cutie pie and seeing her naked was a real treat. That was why we were in the shower. That was a great shower.

We both thought sex was an expression of love, when in fact it was lust. If we had taken the time to love one another, we might have found a way to stay together, but we thought we were in love. We didn't know any better. We both fell into the trap of lusting each other naked in the comfort of our home. Iggy would come knocking, and I would just ignore it, so Marjorie and I would have more alone time. Iggy would eventually quit knocking. It is hard to hide when someone outside is yelling, "I know you are in there." Kablam. Kablam. Kablam. "Come on. Open up."

I've always liked space. There were four rooms to hide in. We would climb back into our sex frenzy at our Fern Rock castle after Iggy left.

Marjorie and I were doing everything together. One time when I was separated from her while at the drag races with all my family, my little brother was racing a Karman Ghia. He had souped it up and was beating a lot of eight-cylinders with a four-cylinder. He had made it to the finals, but we were away from Marjorie for four hours, and I was needing a fix of her. So, I told my little brother, "If you can't win this one, just lose now so we can go home."

We will never know if Gene could have beaten him. It is possible, but he had a false start and got disqualified at the starting tree. That was an example of how hot and heavy we were for each other, or at least I was. I always felt that if you make love three times in one day, that was about right. I thought Marjorie was in it too because she certainly was a participant. I never could have been that active by myself. My happiness certainly would have fallen off if I tried to whack it three times a day.

I was first living by myself in Fern Rock in 1979 when I told Marjorie I loved her; the next day she was living with me. For about seven or eight years we were an item. Well, it was heavy for four years while we were an item. The last three years, we were still trying to piece it back together and never got it done.

Chapter 24

Marjorie and I moved to Peachtree Street in Atlanta for about two years after we left Philly together. We lived in a small one-bedroom apartment, barely getting by. I joined the trucking firm in Atlanta where Bernie Bishop had signed the Blue Mule and us as the owner- operators. Marjorie was allowed to go with us on trips, so we started traveling around the country together with Tri-State Trucking, me, Bernie, and Marjorie. She wanted to learn how to drive, so I taught her.

At that time there were no women driving trucks, maybe five out of 20,000, but that didn't matter. Marjorie was a real natural. She got into that driver's seat and 13 gears didn't mean anything to her. It was time to get going on down the highway. One time she was driving so fast on Highway 81, she passed a cop at 78 miles an hour. I thought for sure we were going to get pulled over that time, and I knew our logbooks were not up to date. Somehow, she got away with it and just passed by the cop like it was nothing. It must be that God loved Marjorie too.

Later, while living in Atlanta, I became a manager for the firm and Bernie moved on after the Blue Mule's engine blew, and we were no longer owner-operators. It got so hot at night that it wouldn't get below 99 degrees. Guess what, in Atlanta there wasn't any air conditioning anywhere we could afford at the time. I don't know if it had ever been that hot before, but it was 99 degrees at night and 108 in the daytime for a full month. That's when Marjorie and I decided to leave Atlanta and go ahead and drive to Washington State, where two of my brothers were living.

When we went out West together, there were a few incidents that I can remember explicitly from the trip. Marjorie was always a hardheaded woman and would do whatever she wanted to do. Nothing would get in her way.

At Devil's Tower we saw that beautiful rock shooting up out of the earth 2000 feet maybe more. All around the base of it there were huge boulders that had to be pushed out of the way for Devil's Tower to be there. We were walking on the path, and it had signs that told you to stay on the path. Marjorie wanted to climb up on top of those rocks and traverse them from one point to another. I told her there was a reason they had those signs which told everyone to stay on the path, but that wasn't important. Marjorie went about her business anyway.

After about five minutes of Marjorie traversing those rocks, I heard a rattle. It's a distinct sound. You cannot mistake a rattlesnake's rattle. Marjorie hopped back down onto the trail and acted like nothing had happened. She looked at me with her questioning baby blue eyes and asked me, "Did you hear that?"

I said, "You mean the rattle from the rattlesnake? Yes, I heard it. I told you it would be safer down here."

I knew there were rattlesnakes in the West. I don't know why Marjorie didn't know, but she thought she could walk on those rocks forever and nothing would bother her. Well, she was sort of right for a while.

The next thing I remember on our trip was when we were in Yellowstone, getting closer to my brothers in Gig Harbor, Washington. We were at the mud pits. It was pretty much the end of winter at Yellowstone, so we were able to come in the east gate, which wasn't open most of the winter. When we got to the mud pits, the buffalo were still roaming around. This was the first time Marjorie ever saw a buffalo.

I had seen buffalo, moose, deer, sheep, and rams the first time I went to Yellowstone Park with my brother Red, Gene, my mom, and Grandma. So, when I spotted the sign reading, 'Don't feed or approach wild animals', I was paying attention.

Marjorie wanted to pet a baby buffalo so bad that she did not care about any sign. She started running through the mud pits over the barriers and onto the crusty ground to get to that baby buffalo. Marjorie was the reason they had those signs. First, you don't go off the paths in Yellowstone. Second, you let the wild animals be wild. It was not a petting zoo. People had been known to fall right into the earth and never be seen again at the mud pits. But Marjorie had it in her mind that she was going to pet that buffalo.

As Marjorie got about 30 feet away from the baby, the momma, who was 100 yards away or so realized that Marjorie was going right for her baby and started charging. It was a humorous sight to see Marjorie turn and run full tilt away from that baby when she saw the momma coming after her. The buffalo's momma gave up after a time; she got back with her baby, had chased off the threat, and didn't need to go any further. If Marjorie had gone a couple yards closer to the baby, she would not have had enough room to run to safety.

The thing about Marjorie, she was a city girl. She didn't know what wild meant. She thought everything was on this planet just for her enjoyment. I got to tell you, though, from my experience wild is wild, and you cannot make wild friendly just because you think it should be. It was good that we were moving to Washington where the snakes aren't venomous. That way Marjorie could still be a city girl even though we lived kind of in the country.

Mount St. Helens had just erupted, and that mountain blew its ash all the way to Montana. My brothers told me that we had to move out to Washington State to be with them. It was the greenest place I had ever seen. Guess what, to be green you've got to get lots of rain, and it rained and rained for three seasons.

Marjorie and I got a trailer in Gig Harbor with the help of my brother Francis and my mom who was now divorced and living in WA. We were living in the trailer with our own garden having a happy life. I was driving trucks again, and this time local, so I could come home and be with Marjorie at night. I got lazy and kind of fat on Marjorie's cooking. It was so good. I went from 235 pounds when she met me to 285 pounds, so I was a little large. Marjorie got to hating being with me at that point and was starting fights to make me hate her back. After she nearly got me to hit her, I got her to leave. She joined the Marine Corps. Marjorie again was a trendsetter. She was one of the first women to be a Marine. I never did get to see her again face to face after that.

I moved on to run the motor pool for the Army and had to travel to Fort Lewis from Gig Harbor every day and cross over the Narrows Bridge. It would back up from 6:30 till 10:00 AM every morning and then from 2:00 PM to 7:00 PM every evening. It was a nightmare traveling from Gig Harbor to Fort Lewis unless I left at

5:00 in the morning, which I started doing. I hid a cot in my office at Fort Lewis and was able to catch catnaps because I wasn't going home until 7:00 PM. That lasted a couple of months. Then I moved into Tacoma, so I wouldn't have to go over that bridge anymore.

Interlude

This is a story about an old man looking back on his life. And I got to tell you, I have had one hell of a life. I'm sharing it with you because you know I have been kind of bored, and the winters are very long. I've got to do something productive. I can't be pulling my pud anymore. I'm 65 years old, and there's something wrong with somebody 65 years old still pulling their pud. It hurts for days afterwards. The skin on my member has become very sensitive, otherwise, I don't think age or dignity would stop me.

I did a good job planning for my retirement. What I didn't plan on was a divorce. I feel like I should go back to work, but I really don't want to. I collect four pensions, plus Social Security coming in every month, but it amounts only to $2500.00 a month. I bought a new house after the divorce. Why does the wife always get the house? I should identify as a woman and get my house. I love the house that I lost to divorce. It was my own design and right on the Puget Sound with glorious sunsets. When this book becomes famous, I will talk my ex-wife into holding guided tours at a set fee. You will love the house as much as I do. Maybe you could rent a room. She has five bedrooms.

Chapter 25

Debra and I had a happy life at first. We met at a bar in Tacoma in 1985 when I had just come back from Europe with my little brother Gene cutting our vacation short. My friend Rob was getting married, and I was supposed to be the best man. I talked my way out of it by saying I didn't know if I would be able to get back from Europe in time. As it turned out, I had a panic attack in Italy and thought I was going to go crazy. Instead of having multiple attacks, Gene and I flew to Washington. Gene still lived in Philly, and I convinced him to see the Puget Sound as it is gorgeous in the summer.

I wanted Gene to meet my friend Rob, a tire salesman, and we three went to a bar for lunch and drinks. We went to Johnny's Dock in Tacoma, and Debra was our server. She saw that I had Player cigarettes. The only place you could get them was in Europe, so she knew I'd been, because she had been there. Gene bugged me into asking Debra out because earlier that day, I had let an 18-year-old who approached me get away without getting her phone number. I had met her previously while I was acting in a play, and she had played clarinet in the orchestra.

After the play we had a cast party at my friend Craig's house on American Lake. I was being crazy on the rope swing, doing flips and landing in the water. I had played a minor role, and she took a fancy to me. At my friend Craig's house, all of us took turns swinging on the rope swing and dumping ourselves into the water. Gene told me that I better get Debra's phone number, and not let another girl get away from me with no way to contact her. So, I asked Debra if she wanted to get some coffee or something, and surprisingly she gave me her real phone number. I called her, and we started dating.

We were living together within a few months, and we stayed together for 33 years after that. I think that was cool, except that I was there for the last 15 years, and I got to tell you those years were hard. As soon as Debra got sober, we had a lot of trouble because we were always fighting over everything. For the first part of our relationship, Debra agreed with every decision I made. I even asked her to get sober, because she would drink until she passed out every day. I got to tell you, that was my mistake. She had been drinking to forget about her infidelity, and the fact that she was miserable as a teacher. From then on, we were fighting about everything. We couldn't spend an hour without an argument about something, so last 15 years were hard. I should have let her go in the Carolinas, but when she said she wouldn't cheat again, I tried to forgive her. I had made a promise to God — till death do us part — and it meant something to me. I always thought we would be able to figure out our problems and move on from them, but that just didn't happen.

Chapter 26

My grandmother came to live with my mom in Gig Harbor towards the end of her life. She had made a small garden. She then brought a Troy rototiller and asked me to help her expand it. I had already made a 6' x 6' garden spot for her by hand right over the septic drain field, but she wanted it bigger, so I made it 12' x 12'. It was hard work, as the soil had never been turned, but it sure was a lot easier using a rototiller rather than a shovel. She planted that whole area with peas, and when I came back a week later, she said, "You have to make me more garden. I planted that all in peas."

I said to her, "Grandma, that was supposed to be your whole garden."

"Oh, please Leslie, you have to make the garden bigger for me, so I can grow corn and broccoli." Still, at nearly 32 years old, I could not deny her, so Troy and I made a 20' x 40' spot for her, and she planted the whole thing with different vegetables.

Debra told me that she saw how well I treated my grandmother. We went over to my mom's house where Grandma now lived to borrow a bicycle, so Debra and I could go riding in Point Defiance Park with two bikes. My actions and words were filled with love, and Debra fell in love with me. Debra and I had a long and wonderful time the first 18 years, until I caught her cheating.

We moved from Seattle to Buffalo. We each got teaching degrees from Canisius College and became teachers. From Buffalo we moved to North Carolina, where we both taught English. I started teaching math and fell in love with it as a subject, and I never went back to teaching English. We met Ralph and Linda Bottom and became good friends. Ralph and Debra secretly became much more than friends.

I don't really want to go there, but I feel like I must. After I caught them in my kitchen, they found ways to meet for two more years. Somehow, I didn't catch her until the very end. I don't really want to tell you about this because it makes me feel like a fool and makes me angry. Leslie used to be my name. I killed Leslie in my mind because he was such a loving and trusting fool. I couldn't live with someone who had betrayed me for five years, so I changed my name from Leslie to Ed and stayed with Debra. I can't say that I ever forgave her. I tried, but when you betray your husband for five years with his supposed best friend, should you be forgiven?

Hate is such a strong word, and I have always wished that I could forgive her, but my hatred for her actions has always prevented it.

I remember the day. I knew it was happening, but I didn't want to believe she was having sex with my best friend. We were all in Wilmington, NC. Ralph and his wife Linda came to visit Debra and me at our home. Linda and I went to the store and left Ralph and Debra behind. We were gone for about 45 minutes, and that was when they were fucking each other.

When Linda and I got back to the house, I could smell sex. Debra had never orgasmed like that for me, but I knew the smell from my first wife. One time Marjorie and I were having a romp and two neighborhood tom cats climbed into the open window, looking for the cat in heat. It wasn't a cat smell. It was from the multiple orgasms Marjorie and I gave each other, so I was familiar with the smell. Debra and I in our eighteen years together at that time had never put out that smell. Ralph must have really turned her on.

I learned from her diary three years later that he was doing her from behind while they were standing up in the kitchen. She was holding on to a kitchen chair while he screwed her from behind. She said in her diary that, "Ralph must really love me. This was the first time he penetrated me without a rubber." At that point they had already been having sex for three years.

I kicked Ralph out of the house because I knew exactly what had happened. Even though I did not know all the details then, I knew what good sex smelled like. Ralph had brought an automatic shotgun with him. I think he always feared that I would one day figure out what was going on between him and Debra, and he brought this shotgun to intimidate me. Now I am sure of that. I made Ralph and his wife leave and told him I never wanted to see them again. Debra wondered how I knew that it had happened. My only regret is that I did not figure it out sooner than that. Shortly thereafter Debra and I separated, and she went to live with a girlfriend. I would not let her back into my house. But somehow that woman managed to weasel her way back into my life, telling me about how she was never going to do it again. Then she managed to hook up with Ralph for two more years. They would meet in hotels somewhere between our two houses. Debra said she was taking classes. Ralph and I have never spoken after the time I threw them out. I just didn't know before that.

Chapter 27

I don't pray to God very often because I know he must be really busy. There's way more of us on this planet than I would ever want to hear chattering away every day. I reserve my chattering to very specific moments.

Once when I was living in South Carolina with Debra around 1999, I asked God to give me a bag of money. Things were tough on my salary although I was a principal at that point. Making ends meet was not always possible, so we needed some money. I asked God to leave me a bag of money, and I prayed for it. Well, the next morning I got up to go to work, and I had to go through River Hills Country Club to get to Loris, South Carolina where I worked. We had stretched our money to the limit to buy the extremely fancy golf course home in an elite neighborhood just north of Myrtle Beach.

I was pulling out of my driveway when I saw a bank bag right in the street, so I stopped to pick it up. Guess what? There was about $11,000 in cash in that bank bag, plus some checks, and a deposit slip. God had answered my prayer. Ironically, the checks were made out to the car wash, and I knew my neighbor owned the car wash. I had $11,000 in cash, but I had a bank deposit slip that told me it is my neighbor's money. There was no way that the cash could have been traced back to me, but since I knew that it was my neighbor's deposit, I had to give it back. I saw my neighbor's wife, going around the circle the other way, so I raced to the end of the circle, and I stopped her. I said, "Are you looking for something?"

She said, "Yes, my husband has lost his deposit bag." She told me that her husband had lost his whole deposit, so I went back to my car, and I got the bank bag. I gave all $11,000 in cash and $16,000 in checks back to her. I knew it was theirs. Even though I really needed that money, I gave it back to them.

That evening the car wash owner, my next-door neighbor, came and gave me one free car wash as a reward for essentially $27,000 in cash and checks. I almost wished that he had given me nothing. The one car wash, which I never used, was a slap in my face in my opinion. He could have easily given me a year's worth of car washes. That might have meant something.

It was not all about the money. I prayed to God again that night, and I said, "God, do you think maybe you could have given me a bag of money that didn't have somebody else's name written all over it, so I wouldn't have to give it back?" You see, God did answer my prayer. He did everything I asked him to do, but my conscience wouldn't allow me to keep that money. I was no longer a criminal. The criminal me from previous years could have easily kept that money. But at that point, I was a changed man.

Chapter 28

Once as a principal in Loris, I got in trouble at my school when I suspended two White kids for beating up one Black kid. In South Carolina we called this lynching whenever two or more people beat up on one. The White boys' father came into me and said to me that he had taught his boys to stand together. When one of his boys was losing the fight, the other was supposed to go in and help him. I told him that it was a three-day suspension because that was their first fighting offense ever. But if he wanted his children to stay out of trouble, he would advise them not to fight at school at all and to avoid it as much as possible. He told me that no other principal would have done this to his kids. Mind you we were in the South and Black kids still didn't have the same rights as White kids.

I told him that this was school policy. If he didn't want me to suspend his kids, he should get the school policy changed. Then I wouldn't have to suspend his kids. His boys had met the definition of lynching. Both of his boys were pounding on this other kid. Granted, I suspended the Black kid too for fighting.

One of my jobs at Loris Middle School was to make sure that fighting was not an everyday occurrence anymore. When I got to that school, it was normal to have more than twenty fights a week. There were three or four fights every day, and more on Fridays. The drama was never-ending. When I left Loris, there was only one fight a week. It took two years, but with faculty and parent involvement, we changed the whole atmosphere into a learning environment. Fighting became secondary to learning. We went from a failing school to an excellent school during the five years I was there.

I wasn't going to treat the White kids any differently than I would the Black kids that were fighting. Interracial fighting was fairly rare at school, because the Black kids knew they were always going to get punished worse than the White kids. I wasn't going to do this. If the policy was written to punish people for their crimes, then that was what I was going to do, follow policy.

In the long run, following policy made me quite popular. By the end of my tenure at that school, I had not only solved the crisis with special education, but I had also helped (with the help of my teachers) to solve the fighting crisis. We made a schoolwide discipline policy which didn't allow problems to fester. When children had a confrontation with each other, the drama wasn't allowed to build into a fight. They received peer counseling long before they would start finding each other to fight. I've often thought this was my calling in life, but I never got another chance to be a principal after that. I moved to Washington to be with Debra, whom I had taken to Washington to get away from Ralph just two years earlier.

Interlude

I really believe that my calling was to be in education, and to help students to change. My purpose was to guide them to recognizing their full potential and revealing for them the value in learning. I would help them to jump-start their brains and find a way to utilize their minds for something other than just baking. Baking (getting high) was probably the worst thing that I came across in high school. When I was a student, baking was all I wanted to do. I know that it drained my potential. I was a B student before baking and a D student after. It wasn't until much later that I put education and learning first, when I got my first official Master's in teaching, my MST. I think that one of the reasons that I was never prosecuted for doing any criminal acts was because God wanted my record clear. I could not have gone into education if I had a criminal record.

During all my years in education, I was dedicated to helping kids find their full potential. I still have students that I once taught contacting me, showing me pictures of their kids, telling me what they're doing in life, and asking me for advice. I never mind helping them through life, as I did when I was a teacher and principal. I never could have done any of that if I had had a criminal record, so I know that God loves me. Otherwise, I never would have gotten the chance to be His emissary.

I never preached to anybody. I think that this writing might be the first time that many people who know me will realize how close to God I actually am. I believe that actions speak for you, and that's how you should show your Christianity. I have never pressed my Christian values on anybody, though I have shown thousands of people righteousness. If it's policy for one type of person, it is policy for all types of people. If you don't like the policy, then that's what you need to get changed. It can't be an individual thing where one person gets treated one way, and another gets treated a different way for the same offense. That's just crazy, and that is not righteousness.

In my 31 years in education, I have impacted several thousand kids, helping them to activate their brains and work for a better life. I helped them to believe in themselves and decide to do the right thing even though their friends might not be. My goal was to get students who acted brain dead to learn how to think. To this day there has only been one child that I couldn't teach math. Everyone else I was able to reach in some way. I will admit that there are some that did not want to try. That was one of the requirements in my classroom. You had to be willing to try. I would let you fail if you were not willing to try, but if you were willing to try, I would help you make it. I chased kids down after school to let them know that they only had to redo one test if they wanted to pass. I would never let somebody pass who didn't earn it. I was offered sexual favors, marijuana, alcohol parties, and all kinds of things to let students pass. I told every single one of them to come in with me and study, and I will help you pass this test. Every student had to earn their grade. I never gave anyone a grade they didn't earn.

Chapter 29

When I was trying to be happily married, Debra would be talking in the background of my every thought. She was talking because she wanted everyone to hear what she was saying. Talking to be talking, and talking, and talking, and talking.

"No one is listening, so what is all that talking about? Could you please stop? Wow, how smart you are, always talking and talking." I would only say this in my own head. I would get high all the time, so I could tune her out. We went on cruises any time we could throughout our marriage. She thought I loved cruising, but what I really loved was that she would always find someone else she could talk to.

I guess that is why I am still single now. Replacing Debra, even though she was a lying, cheating whore, has been impossible because she was such a beauty. I think that her beauty was why I wanted to try so hard to forgive her and try to continue with a normal life. Later, when we adopted Ronnie, she let him steal her heart completely away from me. It was downhill from there. That's another story, and I'll get to that later.

From the time I moved back to Washington to be with Debra, I was never a principal again. From that point on, I taught high school mathematics.

Mathematics is the only real subject left in high school. We used to teach grammar in English class, but that has gone out the window. We used to teach history in the history classes, but that has gone out the window. We used to teach civics, and what each branch of the government was responsible for, but that has gone out the window. We would teach business, so people would know how to write a check, pay their bills, and function in society, but all that has been eliminated. The only real subject that's left is mathematics. I taught mathematics because I liked it when there was an answer. I spent the rest of my career in education teaching mathematics.

Chapter 30

Not to say that I am bitter about the divorce, but I really am. We adopted this boy, Ronnie, at 12 years old. He stole my wife's heart, and her affections. I was left out of everything. I never should have adopted him because I pay the price now. My ex gets my money for childcare. What a rip. He steals my wife, and I must pay her for him. I thought that she would love me more, but she only had room in her heart for one. When he was 14, I had already been totally cut off from my wife's affections. I caught them in our bed together with his hand cupping her breast. Yes, they had clothes on, but that was not the point. She was not even fighting it, and I know if she didn't want you to be touching her breast, she would stop you. I know because I was not allowed in any of that territory, and she demonstrated her hatred for me anytime I sought her affection.

This was why I was so upset with Debra being overly affectionate with Ronnie. It was not the first time she had taken another man's advances over mine. At fourteen, Ronnie was a man with a fully functioning penis, and he was allowed to fondle my wife's breast. I had been cut off and wasn't allowed there. I don't even know how many other men she had slept with. All I really know is that it was more than just Ralph. I can't dwell on that subject anymore as it is too infuriating.

That was the last straw for me. I kicked them both out and kept them out for three weeks. I really wanted the house. I changed the locks and everything, but they got it into their minds that they were not doing anything wrong. So, I got a divorce.

"You may think you're not doing anything wrong, but guess what? I do," I said. I moved to Florida, so I could be 3,500 miles away from them and not see their relationship blossoming as I believe it will. This wasn't the first time my wife cheated on me. It was just the last time I would try to forgive her.

As soon as we got Ronnie, I didn't have a wife anymore. She became a mother. That pretty much killed her being my wife. I was so jealous of Ronnie, and all their cuddling. All the time hugging, sitting on each other's laps, poking, and fondling each other. I asked them to stop because they were being too intimate with each other, but both of them just pushed me further away. When they started cuddling in the bed, I couldn't stand it anymore. The last three years were the hardest. I really thought I was going to leave Debra after our dog Oscar died because she also left him behind. Both Oscar and I got left behind when Debra got Ronnie. Oscar had been a loyal dog and a service dog for Debra for 12 years. He never understood getting left behind.

From that point on there was no stopping Ronnie and Debra. They went everywhere together and did everything together. There was no room for me or Oscar. The last two years of Oscar's life were pretty damn miserable. The woman he loved and had spent every moment of his life with, loyally standing by her side, had pushed him away. Oscar was constantly denied any attention from Debra. It was heartbreaking to see, even though my heart was getting broken at the same time, but Oscar never understood. His unconditional love was never again rewarded. I am crying now at the pain I know that dog was suffering. I am still suffering the same pain to this day. I had to put Oscar down, as he got cancer. Debra was with us, but she had long since stopped loving both of us. She didn't even cry for him. Two loyal lives lost to Debra forever.

Interlude

The loneliness that has engulfed me has driven me to write my memoirs. This loneliness is astounding. I never realized how important family was to me until I started writing down my feelings about my married family and blood brothers. All of whom are gone now. Every one of them has left me, and I am by myself. I am trying to overcome my loneliness through envisioning my past and bringing to life those things that I would have long forgotten. Writing this book has made me realize how truly lonely I am.

Chapter 31

Debra and I had adopted Ronnie, and we also had a delightful little girl come and live with us. Her name was Lillis. Debra had Ronnie, so why couldn't I have a child, Lillis? My loneliness has made me realize how much I'm going to miss the family that I never really had. Lillis would be 13 now and well on her way through childhood. I wanted to adopt her and make her a part of our family. Debra and Ronnie joined together and denied me adopting Lillis. Debra had what she needed, and my feelings were ignored. Looking back on it now, I wish I had been more demonstrative and gotten my way. Maybe if it had been possible, things would now be different. If I had had someone who loved me, it wouldn't matter that Ronnie and Debra fell in love. I had been able to close my eyes to her infidelities before, even though subconsciously I knew she was cheating with Ralph. The infidelity was occurring then, and it was happening again now. I couldn't allow myself to witness Ronnie and Debra in love. When she put Ronnie's and her wishes before mine, I knew I was lost.

I had killed Leslie because I was tired of being teased in school, as a teacher, and later legally to continue living with Debra. I changed my name legally so that I could continue to try and love Debra. Now she was falling in love again with someone else—Ronnie. Who was I going to kill now? Leslie had been such a fool.

He wanted to believe in love, but love just wasn't in the cards for Leslie nor Ed. They were both fools.

I guess a leopard cannot change his spots. Even though I had changed my name and thought I had changed my persona, I still was not able to see what was coming in front of me as Debra and Ronnie fell more and more in love. They will tell you that it's normal affection, but when a child burrows his head into his stepmother's bosom at 14, I don't think that it was normal. Then there was the time Ronnie came out of the shower naked and said, "Look, Debra," and shook his wanger in her face.

She said, "Nothing about Ronnie's behavior is abnormal," when I confronted them.

So, when I caught them laying in the bed together, and she allowed him to cup her breasts with a smirk on her face, I knew that I didn't want to see what would become of that relationship as time went by. As I write this Ronnie is turning 18, so everything that they are doing now can be totally legal. They haven't been caught because no one has believed me. It seems like Ed is also a fool, and I should probably kill him too.

Instead, I moved 3,500 miles away, so I wouldn't have to see any of that developing between the two of them. I purposely lost contact with them after the divorce was finalized because I didn't want to see their relationship develop into a full-blown affair. I left that life behind me and have started over again.

My biggest regret was that I spent 33 years married to a woman who never loved me. She just used me for protection, comfort, and humor, but she never really loved me. I could see that by the way she betrayed me first with Ralph, and then with Ronnie. She was always seeking the affections of another man. She never wanted my affection. The last two years of our relationship, we were just cohabitating. There was no love there. I look back on this, and I am annoyed that I let it go on so long. I missed so much of my lifetime while her infidelities were flaunted in front of me.

As an old man now, the only women that are attracted to me are in their 60s and 70s. I should be thankful that anyone is attracted to me at all, but it's not what I want. I want a relationship with a woman I can love with a family I can love, but I feel like I've lost that.

It makes me want to cry out loud and see if that helps. I find myself crying at movies that have fathers who have relationships with their children. I think that is why I so very much want to have a family to raise. I come from a family of four brothers, and we were always fighting and beating each other up. I know that girls fight too, but not in the same way as boys.

I want to be honest with you since you've come this far with me on this journey. Missing love in my life is the whole reason that I've written any of this down. I am trying to fill the hole in my heart. I am afraid that I'm going to continue with my life and never be able to fill this void and never be able to have a family again.

Interlude

I have become very introverted, and COVID-19 has not helped at all. To save myself from dying from COVID-19, I have become dead for a year: afraid to travel, afraid to see my friends, afraid to visit with my family, afraid to be alive. I'm coming out of that state now and trying to be more gregarious, but when introversion has been allowed to take over, it's hard to make new friends. I traveled clear across this country thinking I was still the man that I once was, but I'm not.

I stand here before you with the revelation that I don't want to be alone. I want to have my family back. I'm not saying that I would ever go back to Debra, because I will not. What I am saying is that I have been robbed of my life, and all the accomplishments that I've made to this point seem fruitless. I am trying to pull my life back together, and maybe I'll be successful. Then there will be a sequel to this book. I hope for all of us that there is a sequel.

Part 2
More Life Stories

Interlude

I can look back on it all now, and I don't have to wonder too much about why my life turned out this way. I was hanging out with a group of guys the other night, and they were all talking about their different childhood and teenage experiences. They were very similar to my stories. That means that there are delinquents out there that were never caught. I thought it was just me and my friends. We delinquents are everywhere. My story has a lot more appeal than I once thought.

All of us at this party were from different places in the US, and we were all retired transplants to Florida. One guy was 72, and his stories were from New York and running from the cops as a teen. Another was from Jersey, and he was hopping fences to get away from the cops. There was even a guy from Kentucky, and his story was running from the cops at a keg party in the woods. All of us had our story of getting away from the cops.

The commonalities of our stories did not go unnoticed by me. Maybe it was the fact that we were all still drinking, and that was the glue which made our teenage years similar. It could be that I was with a group of old friends. I was the only newbie, and they felt comfortable enough to tell these stories. These are the stories that you don't tell anyone because people are going to think that you were some kind of hoodlum. The funny thing was that these people were from all over the East Coast. Each of us had a story about how we made sure that we didn't get arrested by the cops.

None of these men could have become successful as a plumber, an electrician, a designer, or an engineer if they had had a criminal record. It was interesting that I wasn't the only teenager that God was looking after and got him past their teenage years. He helped them to survive and made it so that they could have a non-criminal life after the stupidity of being a teenager.

Chapter 32

I've been thinking about all the friends that I still have from Philly. There are seven of us that got the Mud Shark tattoo. All of us but one has moved out of Philly and into the suburbs or into places far away from Philly. Three of us moved completely out of the area and into different states. But every single man who wears the tattoo of a Mud Shark is still alive. Most of my teenage friends that hung out at the steps made it out and have become successful. Even though many of us are still potheads and alcoholics, most have made it into adulthood unscathed by the past. Some of my friends were caught by meth, heroin, and crime. I know several people went to jail, and then straightened up. I even know some who didn't live at all. Death came knocking, and they had to go.

Chapter 33

Iggy has been my best friend throughout my life. He has come and visited me everywhere I have ever lived. The only other person that has done that is my little brother Gene. Iggy and his wife Lana came to Atlanta, GA, where I was driving a tractor-trailer with the trucking company Bernie set up. Bernie Bishop was my partner and had taken the Blue Mule tractor down to Atlanta where a nineteen-year-old could legally drive one. Iggy and Lana drove 12 1/2 hours just to spend the weekend with me and Marjorie. Iggy made us go to Lookout Mountain and climb a 35' face. We had a great time. Marjorie and I really enjoyed their company.

I was still driving for Tri State Trucking. The same company where Bernie had set up the Blue Mule. I had long since blown up the Blue Mule in Texas, but I continued to work for the firm that gave us a break and hired two young drivers. I was parking a tractor in the gravel driveway of Marjorie's and my rental home. The driveway wouldn't support a tractor. It was just too heavy. By parking there, it would save me approximately an hour every day of driving to Atlanta because I wouldn't have to stop at the office to pick up a tractor. We ended up moving closer to Atlanta over the driveway dispute with my landlord. My pickups were all in Dalton, Georgia. I picked up carpet and ran it up to Lowell, Massachusetts. The biggest problem with carpeting is that it is so heavy. You just don't know how a truck is going to react. You better have a strong engine to get up to Lowell, Massachusetts.

I had to find a particular time when Iggy could come visit. I had to be home and not on the road. Somehow, we managed to figure it out. Iggy and Lana must have driven all night long to be there with us. I can't really remember too much about that trip other than the fact that Iggy was there with his wife, and I was with Marjorie. We did do some rock climbing, and of course we were getting high the whole time. Neither one of us has been able to avoid being high for any length of time. Both of us has had to hide it from everyone else to become successful in life. Turns out you can't be a manager, or a scientist with an addiction.

The next time he came to visit me I was living on the West Coast, and he and his wife flew out to see me. We climbed Mount Rainier on that trip. I was with Debra then, and we climbed half of that mountain without any sunscreen and got burned to hell. After that Debra and I went back down the mountain. Iggy and Lana continued the climb. It took Debra two days to heal. It took me three weeks. As a white boy, I never have quite been able to get away from getting very bad sunburns. Iggy and Lana climbed nearly to the top before they had to turn around and come back. They stayed with us for about three days before they left to go back to New York.

Iggy has always been there for me. He has been there through thick and thin. At 65, he is still my brother. I still call him up and talk to him about what's happening in my life. He has always been supportive.

My own brothers decided to hate me last summer because I wanted to leave my ex behind and leave them and her in Washington. They both thought they could treat me like shit all last summer. I had trouble letting Gene back into my life, but I realized that he had been negatively influenced by Francis. Francis has always been trying to control everyone around him, me included. Gene was easily influenced because he has only part of his brain. He lost a section of his brain when he crashed in the Lehigh Valley Velodrome. I witnessed him fall and hit his head. I held him down on the track until the paramedics arrived. He was bleeding from his nose, eyes, and ears. They removed part of his brain as the impact had turned it into mush. I was afraid he had also broken his neck. If I remember that, I can forgive him for being influenced by Francis. After all, Francis has been trying to influence us all. It has been his life goal to influence three wives, and all three have left him because of it.

After my divorce, Iggy and Lana were the first friends I visited. I went to see them before I went to see my dad. I had to prove I was negative with COVID before I could visit my dad. At 98, he could not be exposed. Iggy gave me respite as I got tested in New York before I could go to see my dad. I drove from Washington to New York and made sure I was leaving Debra and that life behind. I had never liked living in Washington. Every time I have lived there, it has taken about five years before I had to leave. I have SAD, and I can't take the rainy dreary atmosphere nine months each year as fall, winter, and spring come around. The best time of year in Washington is the summer. I have been thinking about going there each summer as Florida is hot then.

Iggy is probably smarter than my brother Red. I've only met one other person that has gotten a perfect score on the SATs. I don't know how smart you must be to get a perfect score on the SATs, but I'd have to say that it's well above genius. My brother Red wasn't good at schooling, so I know he probably didn't do enough studying to ever become above genius. Both of these guys that got perfect scores were above genius. The other guy I met is 45 and still teaching on Maui. He is teaching math, but you must be good in English and math to get a perfect score on the SATs.

Iggy, Lana, and I spent a week together on Maui swimming in the ocean, climbing the hills of Haleakala, and hiking the bamboo forest. Maui is super cool—it has somewhere in the range of six different climates on one little island. I think we checked out all of them in that week he was visiting with his family. He has a wonderful wife that he met while we were teenagers, so I got to grow up a little bit with her too. They have two beautiful kids, and the kids came along with them.

Chapter 34

I wanted to live on Maui and buy a home on Maui. I found several places Debra and I could afford. Each home was a multi-plex, because I knew I couldn't afford to live there any other way and pay the mortgage without renters. Debra and I got close to buying something three times, but every time she found a reason not to be a buyer there. Consequently, I had to live there by myself, and I couldn't afford rent. As a 58-year-old, you don't want to have a roommate.

Now at 65 I have a dog, and he's a pretty good companion. He doesn't complain too much. I don't think I would have left Maui if I could have figured out how to buy a house with three units in it. I had one right in my grasp, and Debra talked herself out of it. I needed her half of the money to make it possible. When she didn't want to do it, that pretty much ended the idea of buying a home on Maui altogether.

I lived and taught math for six years on Maui. When Debra and I were having trouble in Washington, I left and went there. I tried to get Debra to sell our Puyallup house before I left, and come with me, but she had some reason she couldn't go. That wasn't going to stop me, so I went ahead and took a job on Maui and taught there and started a music career. Iggy's the only one of my friends that ever made it out there to Maui, so that pretty much proves that he is my best friend.

Through this journey to get my life back on track after my divorce, Iggy has been supportive and helpful. I chose to start completely over again and not live anywhere near anybody who could influence me to grow up one way or another. My divorce devastated me, and I really had to get as far away from it as possible, so I wouldn't have to think about it every day. Some people can handle running into their ex at a grocery store and be nonchalant about it. I'm not one of those people. I know myself, and 3,500 miles away from the divorce is a good thing after all. I would have moved back to Maui if I could have figured out how, but you can't drive to Maui.

Chapter 35

I loaded up my car and I moved from Seattle and all the way to the East Coast, just me and my dog Ivan. My Buick has a good trunk, so I had half my life in there. Half of my life I left in Washington, in crates at my little brother's. I had U-Haul deliver them when I got settled, and I figured out where I was going to be.

Iggy and his wife had seen the devastation of COVID living in New York State. There was reason for them to fear it. I had to get tested before they would get any closer than six feet from me outside. It all made sense to me, so I went ahead and got tested and stayed in this place until I came up negative for the virus. There's proof again that Iggy is my best friend. He was first person I went to see after my divorce was official, and I left my ex-wife and my brothers behind in Washington. My real brothers are those I made.

I stayed with Iggy for about a week, and then I went to see my dad with my newly cleared COVID status. My dad is in Jersey, near Philly. He has been there for nearly 35 years. I stayed with him and his wife for three weeks, and then I found a place to rent in Florida. My dad was influential in helping me get back on my feet again through the divorce. His wife said to me, "I can't really understand how that divorce hurt you. You were always talking so badly about her; I'm surprised you're not happy about it." It just goes to show you that Debra and I were destined for divorce for quite some time, and I was just holding on to this thread of how I thought things should be, but not seeing how they really were.

I reconnected with my Philly friends while staying with Dad. I am sure now that all but one of the original Mud Sharks are still alive at 65. That's impressive, really, considering none of us really deserved to live past 25, as crazy as we were and how many times we tempted fate. After I left my dad, I went to stay with another Mud Shark. I went down to see Robbie, who was turning 65.

Robbie was nothing but 64. That fucker made me rush down to be with him on his big birthday that wasn't a big birthday at all. It's kind of funny how we attribute significance to certain ages. First, it's 18, then it's 21, then it's 30, then it's 40, then it's 50, then we get to the fives and do 55, 60 and 65, 70 and 75. It's really a big deal if you live past 18 in this world, so for all the Mud Sharks to make it into their 60s is a cool deal.

Truth be known, these are my closest and oldest friends. These are the friends that I share stories with and rely on to be able to speak confidentially. I know that some of the stories that we share are very real. Our childhood together was crazy, but somehow, we all managed to survive and make something out of ourselves.

When I got down to Robbie's, we decided to have a party anyway because I was already down there. Robbie was in the middle of getting his second divorce. Things were just not working out between them, so I was kind of a nuisance. I had already rented a place in New Smyrna Beach, so I went there. It was beautiful and had its own pool, but it was too cold to use it in November. I had to rent that place for a month, so Ivan and I walked on the beach every single morning. It was cool to smell, feel, hear, and see the ocean. On Saturdays all the teenagers and 20-year-olds would come to the beach. It is nice to see that women really do have great derrieres. I don't know who invented the thong, but I really do want to talk to them and tell them how much I appreciate their efforts on this planet to make women look wonderful. After that first month, I moved up to Jacksonville, where I'm hanging out to this day.

I am of course further away from Robbie, but he managed to come over on a recent weekend. And I manage to go see him once a month, so it's not such a terrible deal. I'm still very close to one of my Mud Shark confidants. Robbie is the reason that I remembered spelunking at all. That incident was long gone from my mind. All I remembered about it was that I hate spelunking. I had forgotten that I had gotten stuck in one of the tunnels and had to inch my way out. I had forgotten that we were freezing to death in a

Pennsylvania winter. I had forgotten all that stuff, but Robbie made me remember it. It was at the beginning of being a crazy teenager with my Mud Shark friends.

Chapter 36

I already told you about how crazy we Mud Sharks were. Every winter, we had a ritual that we would enact the day after Christmas. We would first go to Tobyhanna State Park in Pennsylvania and camp out overnight, and then from Tobyhanna we would go to some other very cold place and hike and camp. Then we would come back home. You would think that after the spelunking incident, and almost freezing to death, that there would be no way that you could talk us into doing anything else in the Pennsylvania winter. But of course, as Mud Sharks, we would follow Iggy anywhere.

We took many trips to Tobyhanna. The first time, we just camped there. It was beyond freezing, and there was already snow on the ground two feet deep. Don't let anybody tell you that Pennsylvania isn't hot as hell in the summer and cold as glacier ice in the winter. I don't know how the early settlers made it there. It's a good thing that mankind found fire, otherwise I don't see how we would be so dominant all over the planet. People don't realize it, but fire is the reason we've populated the earth.

I'm not sure how the idea of Tobyhanna started, but all you have to do is mention it to any Mud Shark. There will be a story about how life was almost taken from us on that journey. It doesn't matter what year you pick — I believe we did it for about six years, but whatever year you pick, somebody's life was in jeopardy and almost taken. All you need to do is mention Tobyhanna to a Mud Shark, and you're going to have a good story, guaranteed.

Chapter 37

On that first trip to Tobyhanna, we took a six-man tent. Five of us went because that was all you could fit into one car. Five Mud Sharks was, as I told you before, a force to be reckoned with, so we felt invincible. We thought we were prepared for winter camping, but since none of us had ever done it before, we forgot so many things. It was crazy. It was a good thing Robbie brought a coffee pot because without it we would have surely starved. We made hot soups, beans, and meat in that pot. Everything was cooked in that pot. We stayed in Tobyhanna two nights and then came home.

It was Tommy, Robbie, Rod, Iggy, and me on this first camping trip. None of us had brought a pad to put down between us on the floor of the tent. We all thought that the tent would provide us with enough insulation between us and the snow. We set the six-man tent. When we fell asleep in our sleeping bags that night, we thought that everything was just going to be wonderful. We all had 40 degrees below sleeping bags. That didn't really much matter because when you're not prepared to sleep in the snow, you're going to get wet.

We got there shortly before dark and set up the tent and built the fire out of whatever wood we could find. Sometimes that wood was something we should not have been burning like an outhouse door, or a picnic table. Because it was wintertime, the park was closed, so no one was in the park at all. No one even checked on the park while we were there. We had the whole winter wonderland to ourselves. We had brought the traditional party tools. I was especially fond of Wild Turkey at that time, and someone decided that we needed the 200 proof. Is that really something that exists? I don't know. But we managed to drink that fifth, and my fifth, and smoke some marijuana. We got really drunk and stoned. I think that if you had just given us a room somewhere, put TV screens all the way around us, and turned the freezer on, we would have thought that we had gone somewhere, as high as we were. Each of us was trying to outdo the other and consume the most of everything. I don't really know if anybody ever won, but by bedtime we were all wasted.

Chapter 38

The stars in Tobyhanna are beautiful because you are so far away from civilization that there is very little obstructive manmade light in the sky. Of course, we weren't satisfied with the view from the shore of the Tobyhanna Pond, which is huge, more like a small lake. This pond was frozen over from the dead of a Pennsylvania winter. I was not sure that the ice was thick enough to walk out on, but it had been frozen for over a month. Rod and Robbie both skated out onto the ice with their shoes and were whooping and hollering. They were having a lot of fun, making a lot of noise. They were very proud of themselves for being the first out on the ice. Everyone but me followed and were hollering and jumping up and down on the ice.

The interesting thing about ice on a pond is that there are air pockets under the ice where the air wasn't able to escape fast enough when it first froze over. Rod and Robbie were jumping up and down on this ice. As they were whooping and hollering that they were so brave, I was looking for a log to save them when the ice broke. Iggy and Tommy had run out to join them. All four of them were jumping up and down in unison. I hear a sound coming out from the edge of the lake. This sound was one I had never heard before, but it was kind of exciting. All four of them were jumping up and down on the ice. I just couldn't believe that they were doing it.

We had some different ideas of what the sound was that was coming off the pond. Personally, I think it was "fluke, fluke, fluke." I was closest to the edge, so I believe that I'm the one that knows what it sounded like. Robbie says it was "flupe, flupe, flupe." Rod says it was "flop, flop, flop." Each of us has an idea of what it was, but I'll swear that I was the closest, so I should be the one that should be able to name it. After they had all jumped up and down, hooting and hollering on the ice, I decided it was safe to go ahead and join them out there, all 220 pounds of me. I don't think any other Mud Shark weighed much more than 180. So, when I went out there, I was kind of concerned that the ice might give way on me, and I would become frozen history. Well, that didn't happen. We all survived, and the stars were amazing. I think the only other place that I've been that the stars were quite as fantastic was on Haleakala in Maui.

We got tired of being on the ice after a while. It was too cold to be out in the open, so we went back to the tent and re-started the fire. We were burning all the wood that we had collected. Somebody was proud that they had found a rotting picnic table, and we were burning that, too. Point is though, it was all keeping us warm — in a Tobyhanna winter you need fire to be warm. After we partied and told stories about this and that, we all got tired and decided to go to bed. When we got into the tent, we all just put our sleeping bags right onto the canvas bottom, thinking that it was going to be

enough protection for us. None of us realized what was
going to happen.

Chapter 39

We woke up the next morning and Rod was frozen to the bottom of the tent. His sleeping bag had melted the ice below him, and then the water froze again, encapsulating him in his sleeping bag. Forty years later, Rod still complains about how he had a frozen ass. It was funny because he truly was stuck. We had to heat up water over the fire to melt the ice on his sleeping bag, so he could get out. All the rest of us had experienced some melting from the snow. Some of this water refroze in our sleeping bags, but none of us had gotten it as bad as Rod.

Iggy figured out what we should do was to get some fir branches and put them all over the bottom of the tent. He had seen that on some adventure show and thought it would be a good idea. So, we hacked off some tree limbs with a Ka-bar knife Robbie had brought. We made a three-inch bed inside the tent for all of us to sleep on. Mind you, our sleeping bags were still frozen from the night before as our body heat managed to melt off some of the tent floor. My body was so warm that I actually formed an imprint of it into the snow. The interesting thing about my body heat was that I stayed so warm that my sleeping bag never froze anywhere near my body. It did freeze on the tent floor outside my sleeping bag. But inside, it was very warm and toasty. I was never cold, just wet.

That day we hung our sleeping bags on trees, and they all froze. We knew that we could beat off the ice, and then warm our bags by the fire. The Pioneers had taught us that through TV. When you knock ice off frozen clothes, they're dry. We were all banging our sleeping bags to get the ice off them, so we could use them that night. I am telling you that we went into the winter of Pennsylvania and none of us were prepared for what happened. I would have to say that the most interesting part about that trip was the "fluke, fluke" sound of the air escaping from under the ice of the Tobyhanna Pond.

We didn't give up on our trip even though the first night almost froze Rod to death. We hung out in Tobyhanna another night, burning everything in sight. I don't think there was a picnic table nor a bathroom door that survived that weekend. The amazing thing was, no one ever came in to check on the park even though our fire was roaring all the time. The fire was the only thing that kept us alive, because I believe it was 22 degrees below zero at night. After that, we'd all had enough and had burned everything we could find. The next year, we vowed to be more prepared — but we were still going to do it again.

Chapter 40

We all got into the habit of going to Tobyhanna every year right after Christmas. Sometimes it was a day after that, but it was always before New Year's. The second year we started off at Tobyhanna and everyone ran out onto the ice again. This time Jackson was with us, so there were five of us again, as Tommy refused to go. We were drinking, smoking, and doing all that stuff that kids do when they are out in the woods at minus 22.

I know that most people wouldn't even contemplate doing what we did in the wintertime. I am thinking, truth be known, we should not have been doing what we were doing. Drinking, smoking, and passing out at minus 22, come on, there has got to be something wrong with that. That year we covered the tent with the cedar branches, and none of us froze. Plus, Iggy and I brought camping pads to sleep on. I was pretty comfy even though it was cold. You just snuggle down into that sleeping bag, and next thing you know, you're toasty all over. It was really a good thing that I have a warm constitution because I don't know if I could have done any of this stuff otherwise.

On this trip I think I had pneumonia, and I was hacking up phlegm the whole time. I was spiting into a cup in the tent, so I wouldn't have to leave the tent at nighttime. Several of the guys were nudging me because

I woke them up, I was hacking so bad. The next day there was a choice between going home, because we had two cars that year, or going on to Mount Washington. All of us chose to go to Mount Washington and tried to climb the mountain. Mount Washington is the coldest place in New Hampshire, and possibly on the East Coast. First, we went from the coldest place in Pennsylvania to the coldest place in New Hampshire. Talk to me about how crazy that is.

We hiked halfway up the mountain that year. We got to a point where the rangers told us we weren't allowed to go any further because we didn't have any ice gear. We had no crampons, no gators, no nothing. We were just a bunch of city boys trying to hike Mount Washington. The rangers told us we would have to turn around and go back down to the mid camp where we could stay overnight safely. They were really worried about us freezing to death because we had no way of sleeping out in a five-man tent on the middle of Mount Washington's hillside. Thinking back, I got to tell you, that was just crazy.

We descended and found a wooden structure. It had three sides and a wood floor, so it wasn't right on the snow. The snow had managed to lay itself over the ledge, so you could tell that it had been dug out already that day. Robbie got up late at night to take a pee. He walked over to a tree and fell down to his shoulders. The only thing that stopped him from falling all the way into the snow was that he stretched his arms out. He was stuck in there for 15 minutes before anyone realized he was gone. There is a gap of air around every pine and cedar tree that is surrounded by snow.

I heard him yelling and got Iggy to help me get Robbie out of the snow. That was one thing they tell you in all the books. Stay away from the trees because they have these pockets of air around their bases. Well, Robbie learned that lesson pretty quick.

The thing I remember most about Mount Washington was the gorgeous stars. There was a lot of light nearby, so it wasn't as good as Tobyhanna. I can remember the stars being the prettiest I've ever seen while taking a cruise ship to Hawaii and being in the middle of the Pacific Ocean where there were no lights whatsoever. Oh my God, that is such a beautiful sight. Worth a cruise to see it.

Nighttime came and we were all going to sleep. I had carried two sleeping bags this time because I wasn't going to be cold no matter what. I was still hacking up a storm, so I was spitting on the cabin wall. I couldn't sit up to spit outside the open wall because two of my friends decided to sleep on top of me. That was the only way they could keep from freezing because I was the only one prepared for the extreme cold. The sleeping bags that they brought were not good enough for them to be on top of a mountain with the wind howling and one wall exposed to the elements.

I think it was Robbie and Jackson that were on top of me, but it could have been all four of them. I don't really remember. It was just a mess. At one time I think everyone but Iggy was on top of me. Iggy had a bag that would keep him warm. I was so sick and was coughing up phlegm all night. The next morning, there was a mound of phlegm on the wall that is probably still there today.

Chapter 41

The next year, December 26 rolled around, and we decided that we would first go to Tobyhanna, and then hike the Appalachian Trail. My brother Gene went that year, so there were six of us. That night Gene drank and partied with us. He got so drunk that when he finally fell asleep in the tent, he passed out with his hands outside of his sleeping bag.

He woke up screaming in the morning. "I can't feel my hands." They had frozen solid and were blue. He started shaking his hands.

I had to stop him, and told him, "Put your hands under your armpits, and get by the fire." After about an hour he was able to use his hands again. Gene was too young to be hanging with us Mud Sharks, but he had asked to be a part of the adventure, so we let him. Gene later lost all his fingernails as he had gotten serious frostbite.

We had two cars and drove from Tobyhanna to the Appalachian Trail. It took most of the next day. We got to the trail entrance just before dark. We decided we would sleep in the cars and not set up the tent. Robbie, Gene, and I were in my Nova, and Iggy, Jackson, and Rod would sleep in Iggy's Mustang. We were somewhere in New Hampshire. We planned to hike six miles of the trail the next day. That night we found an abandoned building and took wood from it to build a fire and made our dinner. We cooked a one-pot stew and some steaks that Rod had stolen from someplace where we had bought gas right on the fire.

Gene did not come out to eat with us and fell asleep in the car while we partied and ate by the fire. He later told me that he was sulking because we had not invited him to party with us. He was ashamed of getting so high the night before that he thought all of us were mad at him. We just thought that he was exhausted.

The problem with hiking six miles in is that you must then hike six miles out to get back to the car. On that hike none of us was prepared for an overnight or brought water or food. All we brought was whiskey and marijuana. Unbeknownst to me, the other guys were all doing meth, too. That was how they could hike at what seemed like 50 miles an hour through the woods. They had gone the distance of the hike and were coming back while Gene and I were still only four miles in. I had set a pace that was good for the two of us. I wasn't going to do anything crazy with those guys.

When they came back to me and Gene, they told me I had to go the rest of the way before I could turn back. We waited until they got around the corner, and then turned around and started going back. We never made it to the end of the trail. Well, it was not really the end of the trail because the Appalachian Trail goes from

Maine all the way to Georgia. It's one of the first mountainous trails established in America and allowed settlers to move up and down the Appalachian mountains.

Gene started faltering and ran out of steam. He laid down in the snow and told me, "Just go on ahead. I need to rest here a moment." I knew if I left him, he would be frozen by the time I got back with help. I made him get up and locked his right arm around my shoulder and neck and carried him out the three remaining miles. He hadn't eaten and just had accepted death. I wouldn't allow it.

When we got back to the car, the others were starting to worry about us. We were two hours behind them, and it was starting to get dark. They then revealed that they had speed. I was so pissed at them that I didn't share any of the Southern Comfort I had left. I made Gene eat and then go to sleep in the car. I should have taken him to the hospital. Needless to say, Gene never hung out with us again in the winter.

Interlude

That wasn't the last trip to Tobyhanna the Mud Sharks made. It was just the last one I went on. I had moved on to college and Tulip. I never had time for another journey with my crazy friends. The Mud Sharks did manage three more Tobyhanna trips before the whole notion of risking your life in the frozen winter was abandoned.

Chapter 42

I have some good memories of my father. The first one was sledding on Woodson Avenue on a snow day in Kensington, Maryland in 1962. We got a foot and a half of snow. It was a terrible snowstorm. It gave everybody three days off all throughout the city, so my father didn't have to go to work either. We all decided to go sledding down Woodson Avenue, which was a great sled hill. You could start at the top of the hill, and you'd have almost a five-minute ride to the bottom. It did take you 15 minutes to get back up to the top, but that didn't seem to bother any of us kids.

We had been sledding for about two hours when my father showed up. He wanted to go sledding. Francis lent him his sled because it was the biggest. Dad got to the top of the hill and jumped onto the sled to give himself more speed. First Francis, then Red, and I all jumped on top of him, and we rode down the hill, all four of us on one sled. If you know anything about going downhill, the heavier you are, the faster you're going to go. We were zipping down that hill. We did this about six times before my father got tired and went back into the house. Us boys stayed outside the whole afternoon until the plow trucks came and ruined our fun. We threw snowballs at the plow trucks trying to get them to stop plowing, but it didn't stop them.

The plowing wasn't so bad, it was the sand that they threw down that was bad. Sand made it so that you couldn't go sledding at all. Us kids figured out how to continue sledding by going down the sidewalk, which no one had tried to clear yet because it had been such a horrendous storm. We spent the next two days sledding down the sidewalk down Woodson Avenue. The ride wasn't quite as far anymore, but it was still a lot of fun.

The next good memory I have of my father was years later, in 1971. We had taken my brother Francis's Corvette on a ride through the country. We were somewhere in New Jersey, and my dad had taken a wrong turn. He said we were lost in this farmland, and he didn't know where to go, or which way to turn. I wasn't lost, so I told him, "I can get us back to the highway."

He said to me, "There's no way that you can get us out of this mess without turning around."

I said, "No, Dad. I got it. Turn left at this next intersection." I proceeded to give my dad about 10 directions, and we got back onto Highway 40. I told my dad to go west, so we could go home. He followed my directions, and we made it back to the house. I was 15 and from that point on I was Waldo Pepper to my dad.

Waldo Pepper was a World War I flying ace in his own mind. He was best known for getting lost behind enemy lines, and somehow finding his way back to base. He envisioned fighting the Red Baron but never winning until the end of the story where he finally defeated the Red Barron. It was my father who was lost. My keen sense of direction got us back. I have never really thought it was fair to call me Waldo Pepper, because I wasn't the one who was lost. But the name Waldo stuck, and from then on, my father has never called me anything but Waldo. I find it to be a very affectionate name, and one that I cherish.

The whole experience of the car ride wasn't so much that we got lost and found our way home, but it was the fact that my father had spent the time with me. That afternoon remains special in my mind. I could tell you about 1,000 other times that things were not so special. They come to mind easily. When trying to think of good things about my father, it was very hard for me to come up with anything to share with you.

Chapter 43

My father really couldn't help himself. He grew up in France where it was normal to beat your kids. It seemed like every time I turned around, I was getting a beating for something. I can only remember a couple of them. Most of them are just a blur. One time we were eating at the dinner table, and my dad told me to do something. I told him, "You are way over there. I don't have to listen to you." He flew across the table and smacked me in the face so hard I think it took me back into the previous week. That day he proved that if we were in the same room, I was in danger.

Another time I can remember him teaching me how to vacuum the floor. I was pushing the vacuum back and forth, and back and forth, while he was kicking me in the ass. Each kick was accompanied by telling me how to vacuum. He told me that I had to do it in a pattern, and the pattern was the only way that I would get all the dirt. I don't know how that beating started. All I know is that I was getting kicked in the ass. Now when I vacuum, I do it in a pattern, so I did learn. That was one hard way to learn how to vacuum the floor. Most of the other times I was beaten were when he came into the room and beat me for crying because he'd been beating my brother downstairs.

I can't really blame him for a lot of my beatings because they were caused by something I or my brothers had done earlier that day. We didn't know how to get through a day without getting ourselves in trouble. It seemed like every day we were up to something. The worst part about that was that my mom would always rat us out to my dad, and next thing you know, we were getting a beating. It wasn't some little spanking. I don't think I've ever been spanked. It was getting beat up as though I was a man needing to be kicked or punched. I often went to school with bruises all over me. Funny thing is I still looked up to my dad. I was proud of how tough he was. In truth, it made me into a tough man.

When my brother Francis got to be a teenager, it was the worst. He would confront my dad over, and over, and over. I would get a beating too because once my father got revved up, everybody in the house was getting a beating. Even the dog got a beating if he didn't get out of the way. My mom tried to stop him once. She had to threaten to stab him before his anger subsided. That was how adults treated their kids in the old country. If you talked back to your parents, you got a beating. In the old country, If two kids were playing nicely, the adults would encourage them to fight, so the kids would become hardened. I could fight it out, I became tougher, and a better fighter. I had become a product of the old country ways.

Chapter 44

The neighborhood kids did that to me too. They would set me up fighting other kids, because they knew I could beat up just about anybody once I put my mind to it. The problem with that was that I was fighting every new kid before I even got to know them. Greg and I never became friends because the first day I met him I had to fight him. He was a good fighter. He was pretty much toe to toe with me. It turns out he had an older brother who tuned him up a lot and made him into a good fighter. He could have been my friend, but we never got a chance to be friends. We started out as enemies, and we stayed enemies the whole time I was in Maryland.

The most fun I had in Maryland was when we would play kick the can. Kick the can is a cool game. If you are not my age, you don't know how to play. Kids today don't play outside. You've got these computers now, and that's the only playing you know how to do. Playing with a strategy was the only way to win kick the can. I would hide and not be discovered, and then run in and kick the can and free everybody. The can monitor would have to stay guarding the can, sometimes all night long. It was frustrating to be the one that was "it" when I was playing kick the can, because I always made sure that I kicked the can when I could free the most people. It was a fun game.

Jack Taylor was always trying to win all the games we played because he was the oldest kid in the neighborhood. It turned out he was really kind of a pumpkin. He couldn't win anything. He couldn't win kick the can. He couldn't win bulldog. He couldn't win any of our games, but that didn't stop him from trying to be the king of the neighborhood. Wally was a half year younger than him, but Wally got huge. Wally took over, and he was the king of the neighborhood.

Wally was the one who hit me in the back of the head with a baseball bat, causing my first memorable concussion. Wally was a strong boy. Jack had to give him captainship. When Wally was around, he could trash Jack in half a second, and Jack knew it.

Wally was my babysitter when he was a teenager. Vietnam started, and he had to go to Vietnam. He died three days after he was deployed. None of those boys were ready for the hell they got into when they got there. A lot of my babysitters died in Vietnam, and then one female babysitter committed suicide because her boyfriend was killed there. Vietnam was just a mess for this country. I'm so glad that my draft number never got picked.

The kids in the neighborhood also got me to start kissing a girl named Constance, and they would laugh about it. Constance was mulatto, but that did not mean anything to me at the time. I kissed her one time, and she kissed me back. From that moment on, we were kissing all the time. I think we were kissing for four years, every time we saw each other. Everybody was singing that song about kissing in the tree. That was us, baby, kissing wherever we were. We weren't often in a tree, that was for sure.

I didn't realize until much later that Constance was half black. My mother was always incensed by that fact. I liked kissing Constance. She and I were French kissing at five years old. My mom came around eventually and invited Constance to my eighth birthday party. I guess in a sense she forgave her. Constance was absolutely gorgeous and turned out to be a beautiful woman. It would be nice to meet her now and see what was going on with her and see if she still had that talented tongue.

The neighborhood was a good one to grow up in. It had plenty of chivalry. If you beat somebody, he could call uncle. You didn't have to knock him out. You didn't have to make him bloody. You could quit right in the middle, and not have to wonder if the other guy was going to fight anymore. I think that's kind of why my two older brothers stayed back in Maryland when we moved to Philly. They already had all their friends, and both were done with high school. Francis was in his first or second year of college. Red got his GED before his friends could graduate from high school. So at 15, my mom, dad, Gene and I moved to Philly.

Chapter 45

My father was so successful as a designer that he went from trimming windows all the way to designing the displays on the floor for the Garfinkel Company and then for Gimbel's department store when we moved to Philly. He was an amazing designer and later became an amazing artist. When it came to raising kids, though, he had no clue what to do. He would come home from work, and I did my best to be asleep before he arrived. It was hard because in the summer, it was still daylight at six o'clock. I'd have to be pretending to be asleep to not get a beating that day. Francis was always a brat. He had a reoccurring argument with my dad over the family car until he finally got his own car. Francis was responsible for 60% of my beatings. My mom was unable to intervene. She was powerless to stop him.

My dad was ferocious, and I knew the beatings were coming. Somehow my father had beaten Francis down and shut him up. I'm not sure how, but Frances ended up running out of the house without the car. He had made my dad so angry that he was just steaming.

I could hear my father coming up the stairs, and I could hear him still yelling at Francis, who had run out of the house. I was crying in my bedroom. Trying to be quiet. Trying not to be awake, but my father came in my room anyway. I remember those beatings most distinctly because they were caused 100% by my big brother Francis, because he was such a brat from the very beginning.

I never realized how crazy my brother was until now. At almost 70, he has gone completely over the top and lost his mind completely. He has done so much to try and control me, Red and Gene. My brother Red hated him for it. His divorce sent him into dementia, and he has never recovered from it.

Chapter 46

I was always afraid of my dad until I became an adult, and I could pretty much fend for myself. He never attacked me again after I turned 17. I stood up to him and fought him in our basement in our Melrose Park house, man to man. He was one crazy bastard and tried to kick me in the balls, which I blocked. He then kicked at my head and stomach. My dad taught me Savate, the French art of fighting with your feet. He wasn't trying to teach me, but I watched, and I learned. I also studied from Bruce Lee on TV, so I kind of thought I knew Taekwondo. I managed to block all his kicks, so they wouldn't hit me directly.

I saw the chair. I took the chair, and I ran up against my dad. He was not expecting it and I pinned him against the wall. Then I jumped into the air and hit him as hard as I could in the temple. He fell to the floor. My father and I never fought again. Once my father was knocked out, I was done with the fight and walked out of the basement. My mom was in the kitchen upstairs listening to all of it. She had long ago learned not to intervein.

I can't even tell you why we were fighting that day, but I can tell you it was the last time it ever happened between my father and me. He never raised his voice to me again. When it came time for him to kick me out of the house for taking a shower with Marjorie, he did it very calmly. He asked me, "Were you taking a shower with a girl in my bathroom last night?"

I said, "Yes."

I thought he would be proud of me, but instead he told me, "You have to get out of my house." I couldn't live under his roof. Again, I was being tormented by Frances because he had gotten six girls pregnant, and my father had paid for their abortions. My dad suspected that I would be doing the same, but I've never been as stupid as Francis. I have always used protection.

I found an apartment in Fern Rock. Three days later I was out of my father's house. I took my bed, my dresser, and my two cars. At that time, I had my Nova, and the Road Runner my race car. The Fern Rock apartment was perfect. It had a garage for the Road Runner, and I could leave the Nova in the driveway, so I had my own parking spot.

My father came to me and said, "You don't have to get out so quickly."

I said to him, "I am done with you. I never want to talk to you again." I left his house at that moment. It took five years before I talked to that man again. It really took 15 years before I could forgive him for the way that he raised me. Even though I admired him for how vicious and dangerous he was, I also hated all the beatings that I got from him.

Interlude

I don't believe in sparing the rod and spoiling the child. We can see what's happening with Antifa, and people not going to jail for doing criminal acts. Criminals should be punished for crimes. That may seem illogical coming from me, a former criminal, but as an adult I believe criminals should be punished. As a libertarian, I don't think drugs are a crime. I have always felt that if you are dumb enough to do a drug that will kill you, you deserve the result.

Our country is such a crazy mess right now, but that's why I moved to Florida. No one is trying to take away my personal freedom here. In Seattle we were treated like sheep who had to follow the rules. Everyone but Antifa and BLM were punished for noncompliance.

Chapter 47

Red was always my favorite brother. He would let me hang out with him and play with him and Tracy in the woods. I could hang out with them all day. We would catch minnows from the creek, and then we would roast them on the guardrail on Connecticut Avenue. Red never made fun of me, and as a matter of fact he did a lot towards building my self-esteem. As we grew up in Maryland, he was always there for me. If someone ever beat me up, he went with me to get even. Red was a good fighter, even better than me when we were kids.

Red always carried a switchblade, and he never allowed anybody to beat him up. Francis never messed with Red. Red would always get even. Even if you were to best him today, tomorrow, and the next day, you would have to watch your back because he would be there to get even. I saw Red fight three guys at the same time. He threw one into a tree. He kicked another guy in the head, and the last guy he choked out. The three of them thought they were going to be able to best Red, but it didn't happen that way. Red learned Savate the same way I did: from getting beaten by my father. Red was more of a brawler than a tactician as a fighter. He would let you attack him and then use your momentum to hurt you even worse. As far as I know, he never used that switchblade in any fight, but he had it all the time.

All three of us brothers had become greasers in Maryland, as you had to be with some group. There was the rich group, and I can't remember what they called themselves, but they always had good weapons and were always hanging out in groups. It was hard to catch any one of them by themselves, but if you lived in the neighborhood, eventually we would find out which house was yours and stake it out until we could catch you alone. You never got away with beating up a Dumas or one of our friends. There were always at least three of us when the going got tough.

Red's biggest problem was he was accident-prone. If he was doing something and you could get hurt doing it, he did. One time we were sledding, and Jack was leading the caravan of sledders down the hill by Rock Creek Elementary School when we broke the train, and Red ran right into a tree. I remember walking Red out of the woods and down to the doctor on the corner, and she gave him three stitches in his head.

Red never wanted to stay at our house, so he started hanging out at the barbershop in Kensington Plaza. At 14 he started smoking, and by 16 he was up to a pack a day. I can't say I blame him for never wanting to be home. When you were home, whatever happened was reported to my dad. Either my mom ratted you out, or you just caught a beating because you were home. I think that explains why Red never stayed home.

I hung out with Red all the time because I really did admire him. You could ask him about something, and he would know the answer. Red made a point of studying birds and learned the name of every bird you would ever see in Maryland. Throughout his life he continued with these studies. If you wanted to know the name of a bird, he would tell you. I saw what I thought was a yellow-bellied sapsucker one time and told Red about it. He told me it was a yellow finch. I looked it up, and he was right. There wasn't too much I could catch Red at being wrong throughout our childhood, but that never stopped me from trying.

Red and my dad went fishing, and my dad made Red a good fisherman. Throughout Red's life he was always a good fisherman, and he taught one of his sons how to fish. I was never much into fishing. I like catching fish. I don't like fishing. I can't understand why anybody would want to hang around and do nothing all day. If I'm catching a fish, I am fine with fishing. If I throw my line out two or three times, don't catch anything, and my bait gets stolen, I just don't want to do it anymore. Red, on the other hand, had the patience for fishing. He was very good at it. I can remember eating dinner that Red caught many times.

Red had a family, and he made a point of never beating his kids. Francis, on the other hand, tortured his kids. Red found out about this and went over and told Francis that if he ever did it again, he would kill him. If

Red told you he would kill you, he meant it. From that day forward, Francis' kids were not beaten anymore.

Francis had a way of yelling at his kids and his wife. He would belittle them and made them afraid of his wrath. I have learned that yelling is just as bad as beating. As a child I can remember being both yelled at and beaten, and I really think the beatings were a lot worse than the yelling. Red was kind of the enforcer in the family. He never did take my dad out, but he made sure he wasn't around to get a beating he didn't deserve. One time my father caught him in the hallway and was choking him out. Red said to him, "Go ahead. Kill me. You know you can. Just kill me." Red was about 12 years old, and my dad never beat him again. That woke my dad up to how nasty he was being, but it didn't stop him from beating me and Francis. From that point on, Red made sure he left the house instead of getting a beating, and he started carrying the switchblade.

Red and I ended up in the same class in high school because he had failed. I think that was why he wanted to drop out. He didn't like being in class with his little brother.

I tended to act out to impress him. I would do a lot of things that I never would have done if he had not been there. My mom would drive him to high school because Red was terrible at waking up. She would drop him off in front of the building. Red would go inside and

177

go right out the back door and spend the whole day at the mall. It took almost three months before my mom figured out that Red was cutting school that whole time. When she confronted him, he told her he was going to get his GED and had no need for high school. At that point we had three classes together, so every day he was reminded that he had failed because his little brother was in class with him.

One of the reasons I moved out to Washington with Marjorie was because Red invited me to stay with him and his wife. I always admired him, and this was just another chapter in that story. When I got there, I was kind of disappointed that the house wasn't fixed up better than it was. I tried to help him work on the place, but he really didn't want that. He always wanted to be reminded that my father, who owned the house, was not spending the money to fix it up. Red asked for the money for supplies, but Dad expected him to fix it instead of paying rent.

After Marjorie and I were there for about six months, we saved up enough money to get our own trailer and moved out. I kind of lost track of Red after that, as he had his own crowd that he would hang out with, and I was never included. Not that I wanted to be included. I had my own life with Marjorie. In the beginning of our life in Washington, Marjorie and I were still very close, but as time went by, she started hating me. It was shortly after that we broke up, and I moved into Tacoma to be closer to work.

Red's three boys all turned out to be good men. None of them holds any grudges towards their father, or their brothers for that matter. They seem to be a cohesive group of men that help each other in their adulthood. Red succeeded in raising a good family, even though his childhood was just as nasty as mine.

Chapter 48

When Francis first got his license, he would aggravate my father so much that my dad would end up beating me too. I would hear a fight between the two of them in the basement, and it would scare me so much that I would start crying. My brother Red, being the smart one, would escape out of his bedroom window. He would leave the house and go to a friend's house to watch TV or something. Red didn't get beaten half as much as me because he was smart enough to leave the house.

Francis would say something like, "I need to borrow the car. Can't you let me have the car? Come on, you said I could have the car." My father would tell him no, but Francis would persist about 35 more times until my father would get so mad that he would beat the shit out of him. It was so scary to hear things crashing, banging, and falling apart that I would start crying in my bedroom. I should have been asleep, but with all that noise, how could anybody sleep.

My father would come upstairs after beating Francis, and he would hear me crying in the bedroom I shared with my baby brother Gene, who was sleeping through all the noise. My father would say to me, "Why are you crying? I never touched you. I'll give you something to cry about," and then he would proceed to beat me.

Francis probably did this around 150 times over whatever he wanted that day. He would get my father so angry about something that he would start beating him. My dad would say, "Defend your life," and then start beating Francis. My brothers and I were good at fighting, but my father was a trained assassin. He was trained first by the French and then by the American Army. There was no way that Francis could stand up to him, but that didn't stop him from trying over and over again, until he turned 18 and moved out. My brother would get beaten, and then my father would come upstairs and beat me.

I wish I had been smart enough to leave the house like Red did, but of course it was late, I was scared, and I did not have anywhere to go. One time Francis went to his friend's house and told his friend's father. He showed him the bruising that he just got. That man came to our house and confronted my father. Then there was a brawl right in the street as the two of them went at it. The police came to stop the fighting. They made my brother friend's father go home. Francis never told any of his friend's fathers after that.

My dad would fight to the death with anyone, and he was pretty good at it. My dad took a beating that night as the other man was also Army trained. Both of them took and gave a beating that night. I think my mom reported the fight to the police. She stayed with

181

him for 8 more years until Gene turned 18 even though their marriage was already over.

Years later I was talking to my father about all of this. He regrets that he had gotten so mean with his kids, but you can't take back what you've already done. I don't hold it against my father as much as I do my mother and Francis. If it wasn't my mother getting my father upset by saying, "Guess what your boys did today?" It was Francis demanding something: a pair of jeans, a haircut, driving the car. Whatever it might have been, my brother was relentless in his pursuit of his own happiness. He was always like this and never gave a shit about anyone else. Only thinking about himself.

All my life Francis has been trying to control me. To this day he is a crazy fucker who should be committed. I have found out from my dad that there was a crazy incarcerated person in the past on his side of the family. My dad's uncle had to go to an insane asylum.

I think that Francis is quite insane at this point in his life. He looks kind of like a hobo. He was a super salesman most of his life and had a clean crew cut look. As soon as he retired, he decided that he wanted to look like a bum. He grew his hair to his shoulders and a beard to his chest. Some people look good like this, but not my brother. He looks like he just rolled off a long train ride and wasn't able to bathe. His dementia has gotten worse, and he can't remember from day to day what he was saying the day before.

I was deciding whether I was going to live in Washington after my divorce. I first wanted to live with my little brother who has a three-bedroom house and plenty of room for me. The drawback was his two cats. I'm allergic to cats. I was not ready to convince him to let me spend some money to live with cats when I know what they do to me. Instead, I installed a power source for a camper and borrowed a van from a friend of mine. I spent a month and a half outside my little brother's house, living in the van and deciding what I wanted to do.

Francis had a rental house, and I was trying to trade him one of my rental houses. We had made a verbal deal, and I went to his house to write it up. It was only 24 hours later, and he had changed his mind completely. Overnight he had gotten greedy and wanted all my properties plus 100 grand, which was about 300 grand more than his property was worth at the time, so of course I passed on that deal. Had he allowed the trade, I would have been in the neighborhood. It would have made sense, but when my own brothers couldn't facilitate helping me, I knew I didn't want to stay in Washington.

Not only did my wife not want me anymore, neither did my brothers. My little brother Gene has four acres and could have easily sold me a half-acre, so I could build my dream house and be his neighbor. I asked him. That would have been a reason to stay in Washington. My big brother could have sold me a house. He had a rental in Rosedale I wanted, but he wouldn't do it. Neither brother wanted to make it so that I could have my dream home. Both thought I would live in squalor just to stay in Washington. Living in squalor after my divorce was something I was not willing to do. I have been dirt poor, and I don't want to return to that. So, what was the point of staying in Washington?

For years I had been investing in Florida for profit. I had made a little bit of money buying and reselling houses. My friend Robbie was in Florida, and he encouraged me to come and stay with him even though it would be crowded. He was not like my brother Francis who said, "You can't stay here. There's only one bathroom."

Gene said I could buy another camper and stay in a coach outside. I would have done that if he sold me land to build on. Robbie was welcoming, so after driving across the country, I ended up staying with Robbie a few nights. After a month rental in New Smyrna Beach, I found a place in Jacksonville where I reside today, and I am starting my life over again.

Chapter 49

I was with Debra for 33 years. The first three years we were living in sin, as my grandma would say. We started out dirt poor, and we worked our way to riches. We were never grossly rich. We were just middle class, but when you come from dirt poor, getting to upper middle class is pretty good. We worked together pretty much most of our married life until Debra's father died and left her an inheritance. In the beginning of our marriage, she was a waitress, and I was a radio DJ. Neither of us made any money.

The first place we lived in 1986 was in a two-bedroom apartment with Debra's girlfriend. I was used to living in houses at that point, and an apartment was just too loud for me. I convinced Debra to move with me into a duplex where we had our own two-bedroom apartment just to ourselves. It was an old house, but it was well built, so it was a great place for us.

One time when we were in the living room with no clothes on getting excited, I noticed a car that had just stopped in the middle of the street. It was kind of curious that someone would choose to stop there, so I looked out to see what was going on. Debra was on top of me. We were getting after it pretty good when I noticed the car. What I thought was a closed curtain was just a sheer curtain. The guys in the car were watching Debra moving on top of me. I pulled her down as soon as I realized what was happening. We were so excited to be alone together that we didn't realize that they could see us humping through the sheer curtains. That was how excited we were for each other when we first started dating. Neither one of us had much concern for what was going on around us. We were pretty much just in the moment and couldn't help ourselves.

We were living in the North End of Tacoma at that time. After six months went by my tenant on K Street decided she didn't want to rent my house anymore and was trying to skip out. I let her move out before her lease was due and gave back a lot of her deposit. One thing I hate is when a landlord keeps the deposit. Especially when the property in better condition than when it was first rented. When I'm doing a deposit, I usually give it back unless they've done something wrong to the place.

This began the journey of me and Debra always moving around. One of Debra's complaints was that I made her move 30 times during our marriage. I've never stopped to count to see if that was true. We moved into the K Street building and lived there, but we were unable to make the payments as my ARM rose to 18%. K Street was a transitioning neighborhood, so it wasn't a safe anymore either.

I got fired from my radio job in Tacoma, and we chose to move to Seattle. I became an apartment manager in Capitol Hill and was managing 15 different apartments. We got a cool apartment included, but we only got a rent reduction, and we still paid $650 a month. The day after I took the management job, and we moved to Seattle, they hired me back at the radio station in Tacoma. Now I either had to refuse the job or drive every day from Seattle to Tacoma. I went back to the radio station and made the drive. I had bought a Datsun B210 about two years earlier, and that car got close to 50 miles to the gallon. So, driving back and forth to Tacoma everyday didn't really eat up a lot of gas.

Debra was lonely and didn't want to sleep alone with me on the night shift, so we let two of her friends move into the apartment with us if they paid rent. It turned out that they never paid any rent, and John was eating everything. He even ate my sardines. That really made me mad, so I asked them to leave. I kept the radio job and drove back and forth for another year. I was promoted to afternoon drive and was following my dream of becoming a national disk jockey. Being on afternoon drive was a step in the right direction because at least it was in the daytime. Debra had a travel agency job working days, so at least now we were together every night.

Chapter 50

We lived on Capitol Hill until I got it into my mind that we had to go back east where I thought there would be more opportunity to work on the radio. I quit both of my jobs. Debra quit hers, and we loaded up the pickup truck that I still had from Atlanta. I had bought a camper for the truck and rented a trailer. With a camper on the truck, we set out on our journey across the country. When we got to Yellowstone, you could only camp in one campground with a hard camper. The snow was just starting to melt, so the whole park was not open yet. We had to travel another 30 miles from the entrance to get to the site. We got the last space in the campground which was right next to the outhouse. I didn't understand why nobody wanted that spot until people were coming and going all night long. I was, and still am, a light sleeper. I woke up at every single human that came by.

Right after we parked the truck, Debra left the keys in the camper and locked the camper. I was furious because I just driven about 12 hours to get us to Yellowstone. It was an accident. Debra just wasn't thinking when she locked the keys in the camper. Well, I yelled at her so loud that one of the campers beside us offered his daughter, who was only 12, to crawl into a trap door of the camper and get the keys. Debra was a cute little button back then, and I don't think she weighed 100 pounds. I told the guy next door as nicely as I could, "No, she left them in there and locked the door. She can go back in there and get them," so she did.

The next day we explored Yellowstone, and we didn't get out of Wyoming that night. There was a terrible windstorm, but Debra wanted to pull over and sleep. I found a parking lot where we could stop and sleep. It was a legal parking zone on an old road in Wyoming. We climbed up into the camper to sleep. That wind was howling so high that it was shaking the camper. I was so exhausted at that time that I did not care. I was falling asleep.

I slept for about 10 minutes when Debra woke me up. She was shaking me, saying, "I'm scared. I'm scared. We can't stay here. The truck is going to blow over."

I woke up and got ready to move the truck. I ended up driving clear out of Wyoming. We never came across another good place to park. Plus, that windstorm pretty much went all through the night, so I ended up stopping somewhere in Nebraska in the early morning.

We finally made it to Philly, and we stayed at my little brother's house just outside of the city. Debra proved how gregarious she was by getting a job as a vacation advisor. I worked as an apprentice electrician and learned how to do a lot of wiring. When I decided to go back into radio a year and a half later, I was only a couple months away from being a journeyman electrician. I had to follow my dream, so we moved to mid-country New York. We still had the pickup truck and the camper, so we drove up knowing we could sleep in there if needed.

The best way to find a place to live is to actually be in that place to look for a home. My goal was to become a well-known radio announcer, but that just never happened. Working for $5 an hour plus tips at events was not good money. I did DJ jams at night in bars on top of morning drive, so the only way to make money was to work 24/7. In many ways it was worse than truck driving. I never got to sleep.

Debra, in all these moves, continued to work in the travel industry. One day while watching TV together in Watkins Glen, we saw Bill Cosby promoting becoming a teacher on PBS. Bill said, "Why not teach?"

We saw teaching as a way to get out of being dirt poor. We could barely afford our rent, and didn't have a home phone, or cable TV which kept our expenses lower. We investigated becoming teachers. We moved to Buffalo to go to private school. I got my MST, a master's in teaching, and Debra soon followed with her teaching certificate.

We both became teachers in the Carolinas. I met Ralph, a fellow teacher, in Loris. He became my best friend and later the downfall of my marriage. While I was visiting my brother Gene that summer, I got to witness Gene crack his head open on a Velodrome racetrack in Pennsylvania. I had to hold him still. I'd seen how badly he twisted his neck and jumped onto the track. There was no doubt he had a head injury.

We put our teaching careers on hold and stayed with Gene in Philly for a year while he recovered. We took part-time jobs teaching. My father helped us get those jobs as he knew someone who worked at Philadelphia Community College. Don't ever think that nepotism doesn't help you. The fact is, if you don't know somebody, it's hard to get a good job on your own.

We went back to North Carolina to work as we couldn't survive on part-time salaries. We thought Gene was healed, but after we left, he started getting grand mal seizures. I tried to get Gene to come to the Carolinas, but he went to live with my dad in New Jersey. We hooked back up with Ralph and his wife Linda, and that began the downfall of our marriage. We had a great time drinking and smoking on weekends. Debra and I were renting an oceanfront condo, and we would go swimming and body surfing in the Atlantic. Ralph and Linda would be at our place every weekend.

Chapter 51

As teachers we were finally able to save some money. Saving money is the key to financial freedom. I started selling real estate on nights and weekends, and Debra and I started flipping condos on the beach. After two years of this, we had bought our way out of debt and paid back 85 grand in student loans. I wanted to be a principal and went back to school and obtained an MSA.

It was during this time that the affair started. I was always studying and had little time for fun. That didn't stop Debra and Ralph. I have never understood why she chose him. He was always rude and mean to her. I guess attention, even bad, was better than what I was giving her.

After 10 years on the East Coast, I took Debra back to Washington and 3000 miles away from Ralph. I was never able to be a principal in Washington, and I was still suffering from SAD. I could only teach in gang schools in Tacoma and was constantly getting my life threatened. I didn't want to live there anymore. Debra had quit drinking, and we were arguing all the time.

I wanted to sell our house in Puyallup while the market was good. She stayed there while I moved to Maui to teach. We kept up a long-distance relationship.

I began a music career on Maui, and I love playing music to this day. The larger the audience, the better I play.

I came back to Washington after I retired from teaching. Debra wouldn't move to Maui with me, and I was trying to save the marriage. I was happy on Maui, and the fighting between us worsened as we cohabitated again. We started fostering, and that was how we found Ronnie. I have never been happy in Washington. It is too grey nine months of the year and depression sets in. After the divorce, I was glad to leave. God wanted me in Florida, as I have found music again.

Interlude

When the assassination of Dr. Martin Luther King Jr. happened in 1968, all of DC went crazy. My dad was told, "You have a meeting downtown today." When he got to the Garfinkel Department Store, the Blacks were rioting in the streets nearby. No one else was told to go to the meeting. My father was set up by one of the other workers who hated my dad for doing well in the Department Store.

At that time, I had one Black friend, Nuland. His was the only Black family in our neighborhood. Constance lived with a white family. All of us in Kensington were worried that the Blacks from Ken-Gar, a traditional Black neighborhood, would start rioting. We thought Ken-Gar Blacks would come out and start attacking in the neighborhoods just like those Blacks were doing in DC and all over in other cities in the United States.

The death of Martin Luther King was a big event, but it also made a lot of us Whites aware that living near a Black population was dangerous. I'm not telling you anything other than what happened. The Blacks never did come out of Ken-Gar. They stayed in their own neighborhood and didn't loot and destroy Ken-Gar, which was good because no one would have spent the money to rebuild it.

I have always wondered why when the Blacks revolt, they tear up their own neighborhoods. No store owner will want to go back into an area where there has been that kind of damage, so it just doesn't seem to make any sense to me.

I admired Dr. King because he did everything nonviolently, and I truly believe that if you want to make a change you have to do it nonviolently. One of my friends reminded me that it was what the kneeling in the NFL during the national anthem was all about. It wasn't about disrespecting the flag and the national anthem, but it was about how Blacks were being treated in this country.

Candace Owens talks a lot about how Blacks need to stop blaming society for all their problems. I'm a firm believer that no one should blame anyone for their problems. Problems can only be solved if you work on them. Expecting a handout does nothing but suppress you even more. The welfare system was set up so that Black women could have children out of wedlock and get paid for it. It has created many problems and needs to be revisited.

Every child needs both parents. We need both points of view. I feel sorry for anybody who thinks differently. I know there are exceptions where people have become exceptional with just one parent, but I believe in multiple parents, and I also believe in the grand scheme where grandparents are also involved in raising the children.

I most respect the Indian culture in this country; they never used anything more than they needed for that day. They never destroyed things where they were living, and they went from place to place, so that the environment could regenerate once they were gone. But they too had all kinds of conflicts between individual tribes. It wasn't as though there was peace and harmony throughout the land when there were just Indians in America. There were all kinds of conflicts between Indian tribes.

I like the ideology where you don't destroy the land, but you take care of the land. You treat Mother Earth with respect, knowing that one day you're going to be able to give your children this land. By the time we humans are done with this planet, everywhere we go, destruction follows. We are the cancer of our earth. We cut down all the trees. We clear out all the growth, and we build our cities. We rarely consider letting land lie fallow, so it can once again rejuvenate itself.

The Brazilian rainforest is disappearing daily. It's as though we don't give a shit about what's going to happen in the future. Our greed is encompassing the earth. We only care about ourselves right now. It kind of makes me sick to think that humans don't really care about anything but this very moment. Not tomorrow, not the next day, but how can I make money right now.

There's a lot of talk about the Green New Deal and how it's going to save our country and save the economy. There's just too many of us outside the USA to make that work. Bill Gates says there are too many humans on this planet. Then we had COVID. Who profited from that virus? Look into the pocketbooks of those people that are profiting from it and realize that it's another scheme to make somebody rich. The greed of some of mankind supersedes any good that we do for each other.

China and Russia are playing Risk. First Russia takes the Ukraine, then China takes Taiwan. The belief is that someone must rule this planet. History is full of mankind's struggles with mankind. Please believe what you want. Life is short. Just try to leave this Earth better than you found it. Robbie says that it is the solar flares that will cause human extinction. I think that our time is precious. Take care of those you are able to love.

I wanted to leave you with a few thoughts. My great grandmother used to say, "Eat the best first, and you will always be eating the best you have."

Dave Chappelle's mom said, "Sometimes you have to be a Lion, so you can be the lamb you really are."

I don't know who said this, but I love it. "Live every day like it is your last, and one day you will be right."

Chapter 52

Gene came back to me. He wants to put his behavior in the past and keep me as a brother. Francis hates him now too. Francis, at 70, continues his quest to control everyone he can. Hate is all-consuming, and I hope it doesn't eat him alive.

Part 3
Consequences

Interlude

When I started this book, it was to show my father that I didn't blame him for my beatings, because most of them were caused by Francis, or my mom, but what really happened was I opened all these wounds that my father has been carrying his whole life. I didn't know that my childhood caused him to regret being a father. He was worried about how other people would regard him if they knew how he had mistreated his children.

My father's concern was not with me forgiving him, but with the perception of how his current friends and business associates would think about his past behavior. He was so upset with me revealing his past that I have been disowned. I can't speak to him. At 99 he has decided that my transgression is so great that I cannot visit him. He would rather die without me than to see this issue though my eyes.

I was supposed to be visiting my father in New Jersey. At 99, he just lost 40 pounds and had to have fluid drained out of his lung. He is a survivor and has made it this far. He went through WWII in a Spanish prison camp run by the Nazis. He told me that he has never been as skinny as when the Red Cross got him released from the internment camp until now. After his release from the camp, he was shipped to the USA. At first the Red Cross turned my dad over to the US Army and moved him to North Carolina. My dad was trained to be a pilot, then the war ended. He was not given any money to return to France, so he found his sister, and he went to live in Chicago with her. My grandad had seen the war coming and took his daughter to Chicago with him, escaping from Paris and leaving my father behind.

His sister Julene was living with my mom and her sister in Chicago. My mom and dad hit it off quickly, and he got her pregnant. My grandmother and her sister helped her to get an abortion as they didn't want my mom to marry a foreigner. My mom was so distraught over losing her baby that my father married her anyway. He has always told me that they were not meant to be married, but he thought she would kill herself if he did not. My dad was a staunch Catholic and would not have allowed the abortion if he had known, but it was performed without his knowledge.

It was 10 years of torment before my big brother was born to them. My father thought his first son was an answer from God, but I think he was sent to torment my father and cause him grief. My grandmother refused to babysit his baby boy as he was always causing drama and never happy with the status quo. He says that he had won over my brother when my dad applauded the boy as he lay on the floor screaming and crying that my father would not buy him something he wanted. His first son has always been in the moment and has always only

202

seen life in how it affects him. He has never had any concern for how someone else might feel. His firstborn just found another way to torment my father. His birth was the beginning of my father's downfall as a father.

I should be in my father's kitchen sitting across from him and listening to his stories about life while drinking coffee. I have always loved my father's stories, especially Lt Flue Flew. When we were all little and my two cousins would come over, my dad would tell us a story. These stories would last until every one of us five would be asleep. Lt Flue Flew was a WWI French pilot, who was most famous for his heroic missions over France. He was a flying ace and had shot down many German planes and spotted troop changes on the front lines. My dad's stories would last for hours until everyone was fast asleep.

These are not the stories he tells these days. Now he talks more about his life growing up in France. He wasn't beaten as a child, so he doesn't know where his rage came from. "I was treated good as a child. I had a loving governess and was raised in happy family. I don't know why I behaved that way. I don't know where that man came from."

He told me that when he disowned me. I knew he was tormented, but never did I suspected that it would engulf him. His wife asked me, "How could you stab us in the back? We have done so much to help you." I know now that the wound is deep, I just picked off the scab, and it is bleeding again.

My friend Wally is 82. He laughed at me for thinking it wasn't going to hurt my father. Wally was beaten too. He was raised the old school way. I think that many people of my generation were raised the old school way, and we are all tougher for it. I can only imagine how timid people are that have not felt the rod. I don't believe you can find success in life without feeling the struggles of defeat. Life is about dusting the dirt off and getting back into the saddle. I don't know anyone who has made a good life without getting through some hardships.

Wally used to own a gallery in Chicago in 1980, and he fell in love with Dad's art. He could tell right away that my dad's art was a reflection of the demons in his life. I never liked the demon art. I have always preferred happy art. Dad has all kinds of art as he has been producing for 50 years.

Wally could see the progression, as my dad would have dark periods and then turn right into happier renderings. The expanse of Dad's work is tremendous. I have always been a fan. I have a lot of his work decorating my house.

Wally tried to help us get discovered. He was famous in the '80s, but that fame has not carried into the present. He felt that his old contacts would be interested in a 99-year-old working artist. We contacted people that Wally had known in the '80s who were still working, but none of them responded. It's so hard to make it when obscurity takes over. Even though we used to be somebody, we are who we have become. Most of us never find fame. "It is what it is," as one of my foster teenagers would always say.

Reflection

I didn't know where I was trying to take this journey in the beginning, but I now know that I was trying to get rid of my demons so that I would survive COVID and divorce. The problem is that in saving myself I destroyed my father. His demons were awakened because he read my book. I thought he would be proud of my literary skills and like the book as it really stands alone as a lifelong journey. But no, I was cut off. My dad said, "I have no son. You are not my son."

I had planned since Christmas to visit my dad and stay for two weeks, but all that was changed. I had already promised a friend a ride to Philly. We were planning to share the driving. His mom is near 80, so he really wanted to see her as much as I wanted to be with my dad. I called friends to see if I could stay a week, so I could take the two of us to Philly.

My dad said, "How could you not know what this would do to everyone? I can't believe you would not know."

I replied, "I just wrote about me. It is my childhood. I was ridding myself of my demons. I didn't realize the impact it would have. COVID possessed me to put it on paper, so I did. I did not intended to hurt anyone."

We were not able to see each other again. After I got home, my dad has since forgiven me. My friends all think it should be the other way around, but I forgive everyone I offended in writing this book. Since no one is real, nothing is about you. I hope this helps to clear things up. I didn't know how this story was going to turn out. I was driven to share, and so I have.

I have known some stubborn people in my life, and I realize that writing this book has lost me my number one son status. Why do some people think that they own our decisions, and they are allowed to punish you if you don't perform in a fashion that they require? "I am what I am," Popeye would say. I only wish that a can of spinach would fix this for me.

Made in the USA
Columbia, SC
29 June 2023

19561087R10113